IF YOU DREAM OF A LIFE
OF RICHES AND ROMANCE . . .
YOUR DREAMS ARE
WITHIN REACH!

If you want to marry rich, this is the book you need—written by the number-one expert on "marrying up"—Ginie Polo Sayles. Based on the popular audiocassette course—with brand-new added information—HOW TO MARRY THE RICH will show you . . .

- WHERE TO GO
- WHAT TO DO
- WHAT TO WEAR
- WHAT TO SAY
- HOW TO ACT

. . . if you want a mate with money. It can change your life—and make your dreams come true!

HOW TO MARRY THE RICH

Ginie Polo Sayles

AUTHORS CHOICE PRESS
NEW YORK   BLOOMINGTON

How To Marry The Rich
"The Rich Will Marry Someone, Why Not You?"™ - Ginie Sayles

Authors Choice Press
an imprint of iUniverse, Inc.

iUniverse books may be ordered through booksellers or by contacting:
iUniverse
1663 Liberty Drive
Bloomington, IN 47403
www.iuniverse.com
1-800-Authors (1-800-288-4677)

Because of the dynamic nature of the Internet, any Web addresses or links contained in this book may have changed since publication and may no longer be valid.

ISBN: 978-1-4401-7906-8 (sc)

Printed in the United States of America

iUniverse rev. date: 11/3/2009

The Rich will marry someone,
why not
YOU?

—GINIE POLO SAYLES

DEDICATION

With love and pride to
Little VIRGINIA RUTH

—A lovable child whose needs were great. I could count on you, Virginia Ruth; you didn't let me down. And, you could count on me, Virginia Ruth; I didn't let you down. This book is to you and for you.

Acknowledgments

Thank you to God and to my loving husband, dear parents, and family for your supportiveness.

For love and encouragement, my appreciation goes to Audrei Scott, Chris Greenwood, Louise Kennedy, Rhonda Perrin, Patrick Platner, Millie Platner.

To my private consultees, and to my students—thank you for your terrific response!

Special Appreciation: to Deborah Laake, Carrie Feron and Berkley Books. And to *Donahue*—the man, the couple, the show, the staff. Thanks for launching my ship—you "made a wave" for many others, too.

And to: Mark Goodson and the staff of *To Tell The Truth*; and my two great imposters, Francis Willard and Colby Smith on *To Tell The Truth*.

Equal thanks to Oprah Winfrey; Sally Jessy Raphael, Montel Williams, Sonya Freeman, CTV's Shirley Solomon, Jenny Jones, Jose Pretlow, Carrie Sagan, Joni Holder, Josephine McKenna, E. Bingo Wyer, Donna Benner, Bonnie Kaplan, Lisa Ferraro, Diane Hudson, Tamara Stark, Terri Goodrich.

Contents

PART III
Your Relationships with the Rich

PART IV
Marriage to the Rich

Book Update Interview

Reed's Forward stated we were in our 7th year of marriage; and we are now in our **25th** year of marriage.

Q: *When this book was released, it made you and your husband pop culture personalities throughout the media.*

A. We were lucky to be the right couple at the right time. After the book came out, it ignited such controversy that a whole industry on the subject popped up. This book was optioned for a movie deal, celebrities had private consultations with me, radio stations had Marry Rich opinion polls, women vied to marry rich men on television, and this book was discussed in a class for new immigrants as part of American culture. We were interviewed on television shows throughout the world; and I even became a "Character" in Lucy Broadbent's very well written novel, *What's Love Got To Do With It.* But when we were twice offered a television reality show, we said "Thanks but no thanks!"

Q. *Does this book still apply in today's world?*

A. Environment and technology change; but dynamics of human nature in sex, love, and money never change. Shakespeare is as relevant today as in 1590, because human nature is the same.

The world was turning digital when I wrote this book and it is almost entirely digital now. Books, newspapers, magazines are disappearing into digital, downloadable, storable formats—i.e. fortune.com, forbes.com, money.com, census.gov, virtual worlds and e-books. Mobile phones we had then now have high definition movies, personal digital assistants, global positioning systems, Internet, e-mail, text messaging, ipods, websites, social networks, cameras, and blogs. Voice mail has replaced answering machines.

For Marry Rich, there are prestigious e-mail lists (art and charity), and online dating services (best if in business 5-10 years & check bbb.org). NBC reports more billionaires per sq ft in Monaco; but stay current: Internet search "number of millionaires/ billionaires (trillionaires someday?) in the world/your country/ state/city." The future will *always* change; but **because human nature *never* changes, this book will STILL apply. <u>Count on it</u>**!

Foreword

When a man goes through three failed marriages, as I did, it's pretty much a given that I'd probably let a great deal of time and thought pass before considering marriage again.

Well, that would be true in most cases, but I didn't expect to meet Ginie, either.

Yes, my divorce from my third wife was final on October 20, 1985, and two days later I married Ginie Polo. And I can honestly say that two days is the shortest divorce period I've ever had; but there has never been as much love in a marriage as ours and I wanted to jump right into what I felt was waiting for me.

I've been asked several times on national television if I knew Ginie was a gold digger in the beginning, or what I thought about her wanting my money. Yes, I knew, and I respected her honesty. I like her straightforwardness about money. And when you fall in love with someone, like I did with Ginie, money only plays a secondary role and supportive role to having what you want—and I wanted Ginie.

One reason I have encouraged Ginie to teach *How to Marry the Rich* is because I know that many people who have money are so single-minded that they don't know their way around in a relationship. They need a mate who understands money and understands them. Ginie teaches how to make a relationship work to the greater happiness of both of them. As Ginie has said, a gold digger is the only perfect mate to the gold owner. They speak the same language.

As a matter of fact, in the early part of our dating, I even used my money just to entice her away from other wealthy men she was involved with.

In the past, I spent money in relationships because I felt guilty that I was an absent father, or because I was an unfaithful husband, or because I didn't love someone and felt obligated since I had let them down. I have thought that I had to "appear" to be the good guy. In this marriage, none of that exists and I feel good that the money I spend on Ginie expresses my love for her.

I'm proud of my wife. People think I married her because she's beautiful and vivacious. Yes, I like all that about her. Naturally, I think she's the most beautiful woman in the world. But she is also very kind and helps people in ways that no one knows about. She is nurturing and sincere. She has courage and will think what she thinks in spite of pressure from others. And she doesn't judge you for what you may think. And, incidentally, she stuck by me when the oil business went down and brought some harder times.

And then, I love the excitement and whirlwind life I've lived since I've known Ginie. She's intelligent and ambitious. Those are qualities I admire in anybody—man or woman.

People are also surprised to find that Ginie and I have been together 24 hours a day since we married. We like being together.

Yes, this is the seventh year I have enjoyed a beautiful marriage that has meant everything to me. If there is anything I could change it would be that number, "seventh." I wish I could have been at her high school graduation and married her on the spot! Ginie Polo Sayles is truly the only woman I have ever loved. That's what I get out of the relationship.

—REED SAYLES

This Is Ginie Polo Sayles

I was born and grew up in a small, dusty West Texas town by the name of Big Spring. Until I was about nine years old, our entire family of four lived in a very small, one-bedroom plank house on a dirt road.

I have no complaints. My mother kept everything spotless and my father kept our bills paid; but during those years, we didn't have a telephone or any luxuries. We didn't go to restaurants. At home, we ate very simple, unsophisticated foods.

Especially vivid in my mind is a summer when a girl invited me to go swimming at the country club. At noon, she said, "Let's have fried shrimp in the clubhouse and charge it to my daddy."

I agreed, but wondered, "What is fried shrimp? What will it look like? How will it taste?" And I was worried that I wouldn't know what silverware to use.

At that point I realized there are certain things that you can only know if you can pay money to have those experiences. Experiences that may be simple and everyday to other people were out of reach for me.

Simultaneously, I also realized that the only difference between the Rich and me was a *gap of experiences* that only money could provide.

When I began dating, it wasn't that I liked Rich boys any better than poor boys. I didn't. But the Rich boys held the key to experiences that were out of my reach to experience any other way.

Although I dated poor boys, dating boys with money became an **Educational System** for me—a way for me to learn from experiences I couldn't afford otherwise. It was an Educational System for me to close the gap between the Rich and me, to make me equal with the best, which is what I wanted to be.

As I matured and dated wealthy men, they became not only my Educational System for experience enrichment; they also became my Role Models for business and financial success. And, since business and finance have no gender, successful men can make excellent role models for women.

There was a time frame when I was a divorced, single mother that I stopped dating and concentrated on motherhood, on careers, and on an intense spiritual life. I was literally celibate for eight years, which is no easy task.

When I resumed dating, I had to relearn a lot of the dating and relationship skills I had set aside during those years. Naturally, my core interest in Rich men kicked into gear. I must confess that I believe all men are wonderful—rich or poor—and I don't say that to be gracious. I love men of any financial caliber.

On an intimate level, though, I have an inner fascination in seeing what can happen in a relationship where the stakes are very high and the margin to win is slim.

I have been married three times. There was absolutely no money in one case. After that, I went back to college on a student loan and welfare. I chose welfare because I had a baby and my former husband was unable to pay child support. I could not afford to go to college and keep my child living with me unless I went on welfare. She would have had to live with someone else.

But I chose welfare and I'm glad I did. My little baby was an emotional anchor for me while I earned a degree in speech and English. After my graduation, Rich men became my prime focus, my deeper fascination, my mental game, and a lifetime career for me.

That is, until I married my husband, Reed Sayles.

MY HUSBAND'S BACKGROUND

My husband, Reed, had already grown up in another West Texas community, but under completely different circumstances.

Reed's great-great-grandparents had been one of the founding families of his hometown.

You know what being a founder means, don't you? It means that whoever gets there first gets all the real estate!

Reed grew up in country club life, playing golf and driving luxury cars, even as a teenager. He attended a private, upper-class college in the South, took cruises, and picked up the family business. Eventually, though, he launched out on his own with family backing and connections, and became a millionaire himself, in the oil business.

At the time I met Reed, if I had not educated myself to his life-style through all the men I had dated, there would have been such a gap of experience between us that we would have had little in common, little to talk about, much less to build a happy marriage upon.

As it was, we brought the interest of our divergent backgrounds together successfully through enough experiences we'd had in common. Including an understanding of money.

Reed—like all high-powered money men I've ever known— was undaunted by my clearly expensive nature. Money is part of what a person has to give in a relationship and to give money that is valued is to give of oneself.

OUR EXPERIENCE ON TALK SHOWS

When Reed and I are on talk shows, I realize that an audience gets a one-hour slice of our personalities. It's not long enough for them to know some of the more vulnerable sides of us.

For instance, on *Donahue*, I was asked if I would leave

Reed if someone else came along with more money. I said no and that I'd had that opportunity. And I did, when Reed and I were living together the three months before we married, while waiting for his divorce to be final.

I opened my mouth to say that and suddenly thought, "My mother is going to be watching this show, and my mother does not know I lived with Reed before we married!"

My mom is from a different morality era and I just couldn't break the news to her on national television. So all I said was that I'd had the opportunity and didn't finish saying that it was when Reed and I were living together.

At this time, I'm wondering how to tell her about Reed talking about our sex life on *Oprah Winfrey* and my sharing that he buys me panties and has love messages monogrammed on them. We call them "Love Briefs." They read "My Million Dollar Baby" and "I love you," and so on.

I even have a collection of panties Reed gave me for the shows, worn only once. Each pair has the name of the talk show and the date we were guests on it. I guess in time you could call them collector's panties!

PART I

What You Need to Meet and Marry the Rich

1

Sex, Love, and Money

—The Dynamics of Marriage

> The value of a human being and the worth of a
> human soul *cannot* be measured by money. How-
> ever, the life-style of a person can often be directly
> measured by money.
>
> —GINIE POLO SAYLES

Sex, love, and money are ingredients in *any* marriage
relationship. In fact, sex, love, and money are one and the
same dynamic: the dynamic of "self." Self means "all that
you are"—all that you are in the give-and-take of sex in a
relationship—all that you are in the give-and-take of love in
a relationship—and all that you are in the give-and-take of
money in a relationship. *Sex, love, and money are the three
ways you express yourself in a relationship.*

Marriages of poor people and marriages of middle-
income people contain the same conflicts over sex, love,
and money as marriages of the Rich. They just take place on
a financial level where there's more to fight over.

Why do the Rich seem to have more Richness of
self—that dynamic of sex, love, and money? Because the
Rich can express their give-and-take of "self" in sex and
love through lavish, romantic settings, and with unique
grandeur of expression that only money can provide. The
Rich can afford to give the best of themselves and to
experience the best for themselves.

So, in marriage to the Rich, understanding sex, love, and
money dynamics becomes especially potent!

3

HOW TO USE THIS BOOK

Congratulations on knowing that you deserve the best that money can provide in this life—including the warm, generous love of a Rich Mate.

This book is designed for *you*, to tell you how to project the dynamic of self—sex, love, and money—through the way you package yourself, project your personality, and express yourself in relation to money.

Whether you have a background of money or not, for the sake of thoroughness, I am presuming that you are not and have never been Rich. Don't worry, Marrying the Rich is something that can be *learned*.

Read this book many times. It contains so much information you can't possibly remember it all the first time. Every time you read it, you'll discover something has new meaning to you. Reread certain portions over and over until you learn them.

BASIC TERMINOLOGY

Let's look at two basic terms used in this book.

1. RM
2. Mercenary

RM

An RM is a Rich Mate. An RM can be a Rich Mate of either sex, and, an RM is someone you date with intentions to marry. There are approximately half a million RMs in the United States of America alone. Add the rest of the world, and you can see the pickings are not as slim as some would have you believe.

Not all of the half-million U.S. millionaires are single; but there are still enough of them who are to make the hunt worthwhile. And, besides, many of them keep getting recycled!

Mercenary

People often think being mercenary means selling out for money. It can, I suppose, if you give up being you. But in this book, being mercenary means doing whatever you would normally do and being sure you are valued for it.

In relationships, when you spend your emotion, time, and efforts with one person over another, you have lost the potential of some other relationship working, perhaps better than this one. If this relationship doesn't work out, then you should have something to show for it.

Trust? Love? Time? Don't those qualities have a value? Yes, and, unless you are married to someone, there should be tangible proof that your qualities of trust, love, and time that you are giving in the relationship are valued.

Translate your relationship skills into dollars-and-cents terms for a minute. After all, we put a dollars-and-cents value on the skills and time we give in our profession. You may consider it priceless—which means you should be getting even more for what you give.

I am a feminist in the belief that for those women who spent twenty years as housewives, only to end up divorced, and with little to show for it financially, that the work they poured into their marriage should have at least a financial reward to show for it.

Relationships take effort and time. And, because you care, it costs you a great deal in the long run. What do you have to show for your time and effort?

Place a monetary or life-style value on what you give. Now, ask yourself if you are getting that much out of your relationships?

Be a realist. Even if you don't marry the Rich, you can better protect yourself in relationships if you place some expectations and rewards on your qualities in a relationship.

One woman who benefited from my course told me that a certain man often asked her to lunch and let her pay, or forgot to bring his wallet when it was his turn to pay (and, of all things, would even show her his empty pockets).

She discovered he was paying for dinner dates with another woman, whereas he had never taken her to dinner or anywhere but to lunch.

"You are subsidizing his dinner date," I said. "The money he saves by your paying for his lunch enables him to take her out. This may sound cruel, but you must know the truth. He cares enough for her to pay her way. You care enough for him to pay his. The person who gives the most, cares the most."

After my course, she let him take her to lunch as usual and was not surprised when he rummaged through his pockets, saying he forgot his wallet. She said it didn't matter and encouraged him to order a sizable meal, as did she. Then she excused herself to make a telephone call and left him sitting in the restaurant with the check—and no wallet!

Not Mercenary

People who are not mercenary in a relationship are not superior. By not being mercenary, they have placed a value on themselves anyway. They have placed a value on how they can be treated in a relationship. Whether they like it or not, they have said that it doesn't cost anything to be with them, that they have a zero dollar value.

Ask yourself how many people you know who come out of a relationship feeling cheated. You just don't feel *as* cheated if your bank account says you were smart. Mercenary, then, means you are your own best friend.

The Rich Are Very Mercenary

Most wealthy men and women prefer a relationship with an *invisible* price tag on it. A person whose companionship can be had without any demands or expectations will not be valued. The Rich expect to pay, even indirectly.

That's why the Rich spend large sums of money for expensive club memberships—to buy the friends and associates that cost the most to have.

They could also have the same mansion built in a poor part of town and have lower property taxes, but they don't. They build it in the posh areas to be with other Rich people—in essence, to buy the neighbors that cost the most to have.

And, interestingly enough, when a male RM proposes marriage, he is the one who brings up his money, himself, as one of the reasons a woman should consider marrying him. He is aware that it is an asset; and, frankly, understands value for value of relationships in dollars-and-cents terms.

The Rich may complain about gold diggers or mercenaries, but they themselves are quite mercenary. You don't often see them socializing with people who are not Rich, do you?

THE FIRST IMPORTANT LESSON: HAVE IN COMMON VERSUS BEING DIFFERENT

The first important lesson you must learn is to finesse two elements into your personality. These two elements are:

1. What You Have in Common with the Rich
2. How You Are Different From the Rich

What you have in common with an RM is the way you build rapport. At the same time, the ways that you are different from your RM is what fascinates. You want to play off both of these in order to build a relationship that has enough balance and interest that it will end in marriage.

You must accentuate *both* qualities.

In Common

If you are too different, the RM will not be able to identify with you enough to even communicate, much less allow rapport to develop between you.

So, one important key to meeting and socializing with RMs is to find as much in common with them as possible. And being Mercenary is one thing you already have in common with the Rich!

Being Different

If, however, you have too much in common with an RM, you will be boring to the RM—the biggest problem for people who are brought up with money. Sometimes they can't seem to marry someone of their own social and financial level because they have too much in common with RMs.

People who share a background of money with an RM will want to find ways to be "different" from their moneyed peers to create an interesting relationship personality.

2

Well-Defined Marry-Rich Goals

> As a poor girl, dating Rich boys became an Educational System for me.
>
> —GINIE POLO SAYLES

A SIMPLE 3-STEP PLAN TO MARRY RICH

The decision to marry the Rich can be furthered by a 3-Step, Goal-setting Plan. Be sure you follow instructions for all steps to help you really understand and fulfill your goal faster.

Step I

How Rich Is Rich Enough For You?

1. Examine your own dreams. Your best friend may spin visions of jetting to the Riviera, lounging on a yacht off Monte Carlo, and wearing rare jewels as she places casino bets.

You, on the other hand, may really want a pretty two-story house on the nicest street in a small town and a country club membership. Leave your friend's dream to your friend—no matter how glamorous it may sound—and you pursue *your* dream. You each want different things out of life, things that require different levels of money. One is not superior to the other. One is simply you.

If you attained your friend's dream and were jetting to the Riviera, you would probably have a lonely, dissatisfied feeling of wanting roots and a serene life—just as your dream depicts.

9

Be true to your dream. Your dream can get you where you want to be if you are true to it.

2. Translate your goal into an exact number.

Spotlight the life-style your dream reveals that you want. Now, put a number on it.

Think about it. How Rich can you see yourself being? One million dollars? Five million dollars? Twenty million dollars?

Don't be scared of the word "billion." It's being used so often these days that the word is becoming commonplace to those who talk money.

3. Put it together.

Now, synthesize your dream and your dollar amount. This is your goal of money and marriage.

Crystallize a figure in your mind, right now, of how Rich is Rich enough for you. Keep that figure to yourself, but think of it often. Be sure the number is a reflection of your real dreams of money and marriage.

Step II

Eight Keys to Achieving Marry-Rich Goals

1. Goal Summary. Write a sentence that sums up your dream life-style in a dollar amount, along with your marriage style.

2. Experience Your Goal. Close your eyes and think of a time when you experienced wealth around you.

It may have been on a tour in a historical mansion. It may have been when you ran an errand that took you into a beautiful house. It may have been walking through a fine hotel lobby.

Whatever it was, it meant money to you and you felt a desire to live that way.

Remember every single detail in your mind that you can. What was the color of the curtains? The pattern of the rug?

Go ahead, relive it. Put yourself in the situation as owning it all.

Now, write down every description. Include scents, tastes, textures, sounds, lights.

3. Realistic Criteria. If you *really* want to marry the Rich, and soon, then your *only* criterion for marriage material is that the person is Rich and has decent manners. You don't care how old the person is or whether the person is attractive.

The main reason for this is that all too often people *think* they want to marry, but then they give a list of characteristics and qualities that eliminates everybody they meet for one reason or another—and the one person they do want doesn't want them.

What that really means is that the person is not looking for a relationship. The person may swear that he or she does want a real relationship and that any decent, self-respecting person is going to want thus and such criteria—not true.

A person with a wish list, instead of an openness to what is available *now* in an RM, is a person who is postponing a relationship. *Now* is the *only* time we have to love. And, on some level, we choose to love a person.

And love is an emotional muscle. The more you love, the more you *can* love. Like any other muscle, you must choose to exercise it.

A list of characteristics and qualities for a Super-Spouse is actually a list of excuses giving reasons to *not* love or marry someone.

This can be a mask to hide a fear of being rejected, and so a person may reject first by eliminating people with their "Death List" that executes any *real* relationship before it has a chance to get real enough to hurt if it doesn't work out.

Whatever your position in this matter, suspend your "list" for a while. You can always go back to it later. For the time being, if you're serious about marrying the Rich, make it expedient for both of you. Rich, and decent manners. That's your *only* criterion.

My criterion was that the person be kind and generous. Choose only two qualities that are the most important to you. Only two.

4. Behavioral Objectives. Set a behavior that will signify to you when you have reached three levels of your goals.

For instance, Level One of your goal will be reached when you receive gifts and money from an RM.

Level Two will be reached when you buy an item that costs $. . . . amount and the RM pays for it. Level Three will be reached when your RM assumes regular payments of some sort—i.e., rent, car payment, student loan.

Each goal is reached only when a defined, specific behavior is performed. Then you define three new goal levels in behavior.

5. Honor and Integrity with Yourself. Your biggest ally for success is *secrecy.* It is best not to let your friends and relatives know what your intentions are, or they may try to interfere.

Simply find a new job in another city or in another part of town. Then locate an apartment, and move.

Announce that you have already moved and taken another job *afterward.* In order to reach your goals, you must get out from under their noses and scrutiny, even if secretly at first.

And in order to reach your goals, you *must* take charge of your own life and not live it to please anybody else.

6. Make Hard Decisions that Are Necessary for Achieving Your Goals. Unfortunately, there are some rather brutal choices you may have to make in your life in order to achieve your dreams.

You may have to move to another city or town; you may

have to change friends; and you may even have to limit your exposure to parents or relatives if they are holding you back.

Naturally, if they are supportive of your leaving home in order to better your life and to pursue your own goals, that doesn't apply.

Don't feel guilty about making this choice if it is necessary. You are the one who has to live your life.

You will be the one to feel the pain of unfulfillment if you live it according to the dictates of other people. And they won't really value you more for living your life the way they tell you to.

Be kind to your relatives and to your old friends. Tell them whatever you have to in order to be gracious; but stick with your decision to change the direction of your life, once you've determined it's what you really want.

And do be sure it's what you really, really want before you take these steps.

Nothing could be worse than to cut ties (even if gently) and then find yourself desperately lonely and homesick for family, friends, and hometown.

It's important for you to know that there *will* be lonely times in your pursuit of RMs; however, there will likely be lonely times in your life even if you don't pursue RMs.

7. Be Undaunted by Your Critics. Don't be concerned if people criticize you if they figure out that you are seeking a mate among the Rich.

After all, you are seeking a mate for reasons that the mate has some control over. Many of your critics seek a mate for physical appearance—something a person has no genetic control over.

Remember, criteria exist for them, too. They criticize your values only because your values do not agree with theirs. Just let it be water off a duck's back.

A friend of mine said, ''I've seen men snarl the word 'gold digger' at a woman. Then I've seen those same men go into the nearest bar, looking for the biggest-breasted

bleached blond and ignore the sincere little lady with
spectacles and a flat chest, and they call gold diggers
shallow?''

8. Create a Schedule of Commitment to Action in the NOW.
In this book, I give a daily checklist that can help you
succeed. After you finish this book, write out the places you
will go. Write out the changes you will make in yourself and
put a time frame on each item.

Get on the telephone, immediately after that, and start
calling the places and people you will utilize to make the
changes in your life that are required. This is your plan of
action that can get results in an exciting, fun, active, more
financially rewarding, loving life.

Step III

You Are the Only One Who Can Make It Happen

My book is like a math book or a grammar book.

It can help you only if *you* apply it. You are the missing
ingredient for a long-term commitment, if necessary. You
are the only one who can follow through on applicable
advice—not just parts of it.

Because of the many unpredictable variables, no book
can guarantee an outcome in your life; but it can increase
your success potential if you study and utilize methods
given as they apply to your life.

Accept full and total responsibility for all your
relationships—past, present, and future—even if you feel
you were victimized in the past. This doesn't mean you
accept responsibility for the way the other person chose to
treat you. It does reinforce that you are responsible for
choosing to allow such treatment. From now on, choose
only what is in your best interest.

Safety is your number one priority at all times. That
includes a reasonable mental, physical, emotional safety.

Take no chances that could endanger your safety in any way. Check people out thoroughly before getting involved with them.

Do not pursue any how-to advice of any how-to books, tapes, or videos, including these Marry Rich guidelines or goals, if you are not willing to accept full and total responsibility for any eventuality or outcome, including providing at all times for your own personal safety.

This book—any book—cannot possibly foresee every eventuality. You must accept responsibility for your own behavior.

3

How to Have Confidence and Self-Esteem

> Live your own life your own way, with your own morals and no apologies to anyone.
>
> —GINIE POLO SAYLES

You are wonderful. Oh, I know you may feel frightened and ineffective at times. You may feel frustrated about mistakes you feel you've made. But look at you. You are still hanging in here, trying. That means you are having faith in *you,* even if you don't realize it.

That's why you're reading this book. You care about your life. You care about upgrading your life.

I've been told that successful people are the ones who read books about success more than anyone else. Losers don't read life-improvement, self-improvement books . . . that's why they are losers. Just by reading this book, you are indicating that you are more of a winner than you may feel at this moment.

YOU

You are all you have to work with. You are the stuff of which all your dreams are made. You.

You don't want to change the basic core of you. That is precious. That is your jewel of existence. There really is no other you.

Ultimately it is that core of you that will pay off, because it is unique. We don't want to change that. We want to enhance it. We want to mine it, refine it, upgrade it, polish

17

it, package it, and market it for the relationships *you* want.

If you don't marry the Rich, I want it to be your choice—because you changed your mind—but not because you never had a chance, never knew how to make the best of what you have.

And either way, you win, because you emerge a confident person, comfortable with you, fully feeling how wonderful I already know you are.

THE RICH MYSTIQUE OF CONFIDENCE

You will feel more wonderful as you learn how to have confidence.

Confidence in a woman has been tested as the quality that appeals to men second only to beauty, according to Dr. Joyce Brothers in her book, *What Every Woman Should Know About Men.*

In my observation, confidence is the quality in a man that most attracts Rich women.

What Is Confidence?

Confidence means that you know what you are doing in a given situation. You are *sure* of what you're doing.

It doesn't matter if it's driving a car or flirting, confidence only comes when you've done something over and over enough times and made enough mistakes that you finally learn how to do it right. Then you do it automatically and you don't have to think about it anymore—that's confidence!

If you don't feel confident in a situation, then confront it and deliberately practice, practice, *practice* doing whatever it is you don't feel sure of until you do feel sure—confident.

If you don't feel confident, practice the following behavior that researchers have determined successfully exudes confidence.

1. Posture

Posture tells the world how to treat you, from sight alone. This is one of the most important principles I've been teaching for more than five years. People can tell from your posture if you are fearful, sick, tired, unhappy, excited, feeling like a loser or like a winner.

Posture is the single most important body language there is.

Just let a man try looking macho with slumped shoulders! Erectness is confident-looking, manly, authoritative, sexy.

Posture talks all the time, even when you don't. People will believe what your posture tells them you are, more than they will what your clothes tell them you are.

2. Grooming

One of the first indications that a person's morale is dropping is when daily grooming habits slip. The more fastidious your grooming, the more confidence you project.

3. Eye Contact

Practice looking people directly in the eye, even when you are just walking in a shopping mall. Eye contact helps you establish a position of confidence in the minds of others.

4. Voice

Let your voice carry just a note of anticipation. Sound as if you are expecting wonderful interaction with each person you talk to. Enthusiasm and humor can be projected in a gentle way. It doesn't have to be loud. Humor is an attitude that projects an easy tolerance of the world around you.

5. Facial Expression

An interesting face is more attractive than a handsome or beautiful face. How do you have an interesting face? By having an interest*ed* face. A bored face looks boring.

The most perfect features in the world can't hold the interest of the opposite sex unless there is life and energy in the face.

Anytime you look at something, if you think about what you *like* about it, then your face will carry a glow and your eyes will shine.

If you look at something and immediately think about what you don't like about it, then your face takes on a slightly sour look and your eyes dull under a frown.

6. Happiness
I call this The Attraction Principle. Happiness attracts. It magnetizes people to you. This world is so hungry and starved for happiness that if you have it, they want to be near you, to let you shine on them. They feel you must be special to have a happy life.

What if you're not happy? Fake it. It's a funny thing, but happiness behavior breeds happiness itself. Happiness becomes a habit and then a way of life. Happiness creates its own immune system against many ills of life.

7. Energetic Walk
Walk with energy and purpose. Don't amble. Wear an expression of joy on your face. Greet people casually, in passing, with direct eye contact, smiles, and sometimes a brief, warm, but impersonal "Hello" or "Hi." Continue on your way. Do not try to make a relationship out of it.

8. Center Doors
It seems that confident people enter buildings through the centermost doors of a building, whereas less confident people tend to enter buildings through the doors closest to the walls.

9. Center Paths
Similarly, less confident people walk closer to walls in hallways and on sidewalks, whereas more confident people

walk farther away from the walls and more centrally in hallways and on sidewalks.

10. Stand 16 to 19 Inches Distant

Less confident people tend to stand too far away from people or much too close to them. More confident people stand between 16 and 19 inches from someone's face.

Buy an inexpensive cloth tape measure at a fabric shop and practice walking to a mirror. Stop walking at the point where you feel comfortable (remember, though, you may feel more comfortable with *you* than with others).

Measure the distance you stand from your reflection. If it is more than 8 inches, move forward until you are standing 8 inches from the mirror. Your mirror reflects an equal 8 inches distance, which creates the impression of 16 inches. Practice doing this over and over until you can stop automatically at about 16 inches from someone.

11. Shoulder to Shoulder

When joining a circle of people who are talking to each other, confident people move *exactly* into the circle, standing just about shoulder to shoulder (discounting height differences) with those on either side.

Less confident people who join the circle stand just a fraction behind those on either side. They may not be noticeably out of the circle, but they are psychologically not placing themselves fully in the circle as an equal.

Such standing choices trigger subtle cues of whether or not you fit in and feel confident doing so. Force yourself.

12. Have One Genuine Manner

Have one genuine manner that is the same at all times with people of any socioeconomic class.

Select three people this week with whom you will initiate a conversation.

One person you select should be someone you don't feel

intimidated by at all. Maybe you even feel a little superior to that person.

The second person you select should be someone you feel comfortable with, someone you consider an equal.

The third person you select should be someone who seems above you; perhaps you feel a little inferior to that person, or self-conscious. It's a person you've always wanted to impress.

Now. Practice talking to each of these three people—not just a comment, but a full-fledged conversation—and use the *same* subject, *same* body language, *same* facial expressions.

Having one genuine manner will give you freedom from phoniness and self-consciousness and add to your attraction of RMs immeasurably.

Only those people who have no breeding whatsoever act rude, cold, haughty, or save their *best* behavior for people who are Rich or "somebody."

The way *you* behave from now on is to practice a warm, cheerful manner with everybody.

(a) *Body as Buffer*
—Confident people don't angle their bodies away from someone at the same time they are talking to them, using their bodies as a buffer. They stand facing them.

(b) *Sitting at Tables*
—When alone, people who lack confidence will choose tables that are not in the center of the room.

—Even if alone, confident people want the centermost tables in the dining areas or eating areas of outdoor cafes.

—Less confident people choose the chair that puts their backs to the main action of the room or dining area.

—Confident people choose the chair that allows them to fully face the most action and to be seen by the most people.

(1) Packages
—Less confident people fill empty chairs around them with packages, preventing anyone from sitting next to them.

—More confident people put their packages on the floor, next to them, leaving empty chairs as a "possibility" for someone to fill (even if no one does).

(2) Props
—Less confident people tend to bury themselves in a book or newspaper (if married, this doesn't mean the same thing).

—Confident people may or may not have a book as a prop, but usually not. If so, they use it sparingly, pausing to glance around and interact casually with people.

In other words, less confident people are also less sociable. Normally, they are not as happy and may be inclined to cynicism. All this can be resolved through learning the skills in this entire section. And you learn by *practicing* the skills.

13. Initiate Talk

Confident people aren't afraid of being misinterpreted by simple greetings or casual friendliness.

People lacking confidence are afraid they will seem as if they are desperate and that they will be interpreted as coming on to someone if they speak or behave in a friendly way.

As long as you are in a safe situation, speak and interact with people.

I like to believe that inside every person is a millionaire just waiting to be inspired. Maybe you're the one who can trigger the goal, by treating everyone as if they are a millionaire.

Live your own life your own way, with your own morals and no apologies to anyone.

At the same time, be a charmer of happy interaction for people you meet. When you talk to someone, you are recognizing that person. You consider the person worthwhile. That's a nice, daily gift.

14. Limit Talk

Although you talk to people, you do not linger. Do not initiate more than 3 to 5 sentences with one person.

If nothing takes, so what? You are not just talking to people you want a relationship with. You are talking to people, period. You are talking to people who seem basically safe and sane.

If you keep trying to make a relationship out of a greeting, you can seem pushy. Accept it as a bright spot in your day, limit your talk, and move on to other people.

15. Leave First

Be the first to end any social conversation with an RM and to move away. Your life is full and you have things to do. You are not hanging onto the moment because your life is empty and you are waiting for this person to make it important for you. If this is not true for you, yet (and we're trying to fix that), act this way anyway.

Once you have indicated you are leaving, leave. You lose effectiveness if you talk about going but stay.

16. Positive Self-Talk

Always, always, always be on your side if you make a mistake. You may say a brief, "Sorry. My mistake," but never agree with negatives others may say to you about you!

Joan Collins was quoted in *Parade* magazine October 6, 1985, as saying, "Show me a person who hasn't made any mistakes and I'll show you a person who hasn't achieved very much.'' Make that your motto as you grow through your mistakes.

17. Positive Talk About Self

Choose your words carefully about yourself. If you spill milk on the floor when you are at home alone, don't say, ''Oh, graceful!'' or ''Dummy!''

You wouldn't say that to a guest who spilled milk at your house. You would say, ''Oh, it's nothing. Don't worry about it.'' Well, say those very words to precious little you, who has only you to look to.

18. No Isolation Devices

Earphones are isolation devices. They say, ''Don't bother me. I'm busy. What I am listening to is more important to me than meeting people and having relationships.''

This is true of burying your head in a book or magazine. If you carry one as a prop, that's okay, as long as you look up from it and interact with people. Also, make the title interesting enough to stimulate questions from someone nearby.

19. Comfortable with Self

Who is the most important person in your life? You are. And you are with you all the time. Don't judge you by someone else's descriptions. Choose your own, happy self-descriptions (see Chapter 28).

Once you upgrade the messages you are sending about yourself through the improvements you will learn in this book, you can begin getting the response from people that you want. Get all the obstacles out of the way as quickly as possible so you can feel comfortable with yourself.

20. Not Upset If Not Knowing Something

Have you ever seen film coverage of Queen Elizabeth II or the Pope visiting a country? When they visit, they tour factories, and witness traditions they know nothing about.

Do they become embarrassed or feel that they are less a person or confess to being stupid for not knowing it?

No, indeed. They have learned that there is no way they can possibly know something they haven't been exposed to (which is the only gap between you and the Rich). They know there is no shame in their lack of knowledge, even though they are the Queen and the Pope!

They rightly consider this experience to be the opportunity that will expose them to new information. They enjoy it as such. So, they approach everything with a mild manner that expects to be told about it all. They inquire without the slightest embarrassment. They respond with interest.

Don't dwell on the fact that you do or don't know something. Smile and take the new in stride with interest.

21. Easy Friendliness
Pass people and casually say "Hi" without pausing to see if they say anything back. That's the best method. Just speak, pass, and don't try to make anything out of it. Don't wait for response or approval.

22. Undismayed by Rejection
The more confident people are also more successful in relationships because they realize that success in relationships is a numbers game. They know that a certain percentage of the RMs they meet and strongly desire won't work out.

The relationships that don't take are not a personal ego failure for them. Instead, they play the odds by increasing the number of RM relationships in their lives.

23. Not Easily Intimidated
More confident people develop techniques that counter intimidation. For example, learn how to handle salespeople with a kind friendliness that keeps you in control. You don't have to explain, and don't.

Never be rude, and if they become rude themselves, or try

to intimidate you, look the salesperson directly in the eye, smile, and say, "Thank you. I'll let you know if I see something."

If the salesperson persists, don't act flustered. Stay serene and ask *without* smiling, "What is your name?" The salesperson may answer, "John." You say, "Thank you, John. I'll let you know if I see something."

Then continue looking, unhurriedly. Dress up when you do go Desire Shopping (see Chapter 27). Look as good as you possibly can for your own feelings of strength.

Deliberately Work on Your Confidence

Write down as many situations as you can think of that are uncomfortable for you. Then choose five situations at a time to work on.

(a) Confront each in your mind.
(b) Go through a practice situation with your mirror or with a video camera if you have one.
(c) Role-play the situation with someone.
(d) If there is no one, write it out.

BUILD A RICH SELF-ESTEEM

You will only rise as high as your comfort level; so you want to begin elevating your comfort level with price levels that are common to the Rich. You do this through a method I refer to as Desire Shopping.

1. Try on clothing that costs at least $1000—and more! You may have to practice just going to a shop for several days until you finally work up the courage to try the clothes on.

It's not the clothes that will be that much different, remember. It's the price that is different and whether or not you would ever spend that much is insignificant. It's that you want to *be able to.* That is your goal. *Do not skip this step.*

(a) *See* them on your body in the fitting-room mirror. Look at yourself, long and hard.
(b) *Feel* how it feels. Drink in every detail of the way you look and how you feel.
(c) Learn the labels that have these prices.

2. Try on good jewelry—fine watches, rings, diamond necklaces. Ask for the most expensive.

3. Go to fine car showrooms. Get inside the luxury cars and be like a little sponge, soaking up the feeling of quality.

4. Treat yourself first-class. Stop treating yourself as if you are second-class in any way. Even in ordinary ways, give yourself the best that you would give anyone else.

If you have fine china or expensive towels and sheets that you only use for guests, pull them out and begin using them yourself. No longer treat yourself as if you should use the cracked pottery.

5. If you have no fine china, buy yourself one plate, one cup, one saucer in fine china. Buy one crystal glass and a cloth napkin and use all of these every single day just for yourself. Very good pieces can often be bought for a song at junk stores, secondhand stores, and some antique shops.

6. Buy yourself some small luxury item that represents the life-style you want. Yes, it may be a little expensive— but it is a symbol of the life-style you want. It can be a pen or a wallet or even a Rigaud candle that I've been told Prince Charles burns for the fragrance.

7. In all insignificant, everyday matters, *choose* to be bodily close to the most expensive objects.

One simple exercise that seems strange—but *do it anyway*—is that, even on the level of something as mundane as walking between two cars in the parking lot—or parking your own car in a parking lot—*choose* to walk between or park between the two nicest, most expensive cars you see.

For instance, park your car between, say, a Cadillac and a Mercedes, rather than between a bashed-in clunker and a broken down pickup (even though you may be driving a clunker yourself!).

It is this "choosing" on the tiniest level to position yourself, bodily, next to *only the best* that develops what the Rich consider "discriminating taste."

Knowing the Best

Discriminating taste means that you are "aware" of quality, aware of the best in life. By standing, walking, parking, just constantly positioning yourself, bodily, next to the best, you are constantly reflecting a stronger sense of self-worth.

Once you feel comfortable with luxury and realize that the most expensive objects in the world are inferior to you, then your self-esteem will enter the same comfort level and mental plane as the Rich.

4

Changing Your Image

> Change your appearance and change what you do
> with your time—and your life *will* change. You're
> more in control than you think.
>
> —GINIE POLO SAYLES

Even Cinderella had to have a makeover!

If there is a disparity in image—how you see yourself (or want to see yourself) as opposed to how you really are, begin making some changes to close the gap.

Change as many things about yourself as you can. It's not that there is anything wrong with you, but if you don't change yourself in several ways, you won't feel different.

If you don't feel different, you don't act differently—and then, your life doesn't change.

CHANGE CREATES EXCITEMENT

Change creates excitement and excitement has been shown to be the "chemistry of love." People fall in love more during a change that creates a sense of excitement. This can be a change in weather or a change in life-style.

You automatically project a new sense of excitement about yourself from the changes you are making and this new excitement can attract love!

Anytime your life feels stale, all you have to do is to: (1) Change your appearance in some way; and (2) change what you do with your time. And your life *will* change. You're more in control than you think.

CHANGE YOUR NAME

Changing your feather can even mean changing your
name—literally—if your name is dowdy or doesn't project
the sense of excitement and romance you would like it to.
Look up names or choose the name of a historical figure or
celebrity whose image you would like to project.

Hollywood has known for years that there is something in
a name that has a ring of success to it. Think of Cary Grant
instead of Archibald Leach and Marilyn Monroe instead of
Norma Jean Baker. Make it a name that means success to
you.

According to *Time* magazine, December 15, 1986, Cary
Grant said that when he was assigned his name it changed
his life. He studied it and asked himself how he thought a
''Cary Grant'' would act and be. He said he began to act the
way the name sounded to him, and that after a while he
wasn't acting anymore. He really was Cary Grant. For a
man who ran away from home at age thirteen and lived as
a circus acrobat, I personally do not believe Prince Charles
could convey more dignity and elegance than Cary Grant,
who did so by living up to a new name.

Change your name if it helps you feel special, new.

CHANGE YOUR CAR

If your car is a practical little car, try to get a small
foreign sports car or older exclusive car as a *second* car,
unless you can get a new one.

I had a bright chartreuse 1973 MG midget and it was a
real attention-getter with the top down. Plus there are small
sports car enthusiasts who will go out of their way to meet
you and talk about their love of the cars.

I emphasize that you should only make it a second car
because you can spend half your time pushing it home. You
can meet men that way, yes, but, you're not exactly in the

mood if you're a half-broke single. Your sports car is for cruising in the rich neighborhood where you now live.

As I write this, I am reminded of a woman who attended my first *How to Marry the Rich* seminar. A week later, I walked into my *How to Meet Men* seminar and didn't recognize her as she called to me with excitement.

"Ginie!" she said. "Since I took your *Marry Rich* class last week, I've lost a few pounds, lightened my hair four shades. I'm looking for a sports car, I've changed my name from Berta to Gentry—and—" she added, triumphantly, "a man just sent me flowers!"

All the changes she made resulted in an excitement about her life. The new excitement she felt plus the *ways* that she changed resulted in her getting the attention of a man she wanted to notice her.

CHANGE YOUR BODY

Changing your feather includes taking care of your body. Jog or walk in Rich neighborhoods and on their neighborhood jogging tracks. Wear bright clothing that lets you get noticed. Casually glance and smile at people. You can even toss a "Hi." Just be sure you keep going and stay casual.

Join a YMCA in a posh neighborhood, and work out with weights. Go to these places at different hours of the day—during *daylight hours only*—for several weeks to see who comes around during certain hours.

Learn to make quiet small talk with people who otherwise will go through their paces as if no one is in the room. What's the good of going if you don't find a way to interact?

Whether outdoors or indoors, do not wear earplugs and a Walkman. These are "isolation devices" that say, "Don't bother me. I'm busy."

Even though you're in a rich neighborhood, always follow safety precautions for yourself. Carry a can of mace, if it's allowed in your state, and don't *ever* go off with someone you meet just because you think you've met someone Rich. *Safety is your first responsibility to yourself.*

CHANGE YOUR AWARENESS

You don't have to be a health food nut—although, if you are, good for you! I was at one time and the benefits were great.

Being wined and dined by the Rich, however, lead you into some exquisite restaurants with noted chefs and tempting menus that you want to sample.

Unless your doctor says otherwise, I think you'll be basically okay if you stay aware of the four major food groups in your daily choices. The four major food groups are: (1) Dairy foods; (2) meats; (3) vegetables, and fruits, and (4) breads and cereals. Every one of these items will be expensively and deliciously represented on exclusive restaurant menus!

Vicon-C vitamins are the best vitamins I've ever taken. Whenever I take the time to take them three times a day, I always receive compliments on my complexion (always!). My very own nails have grown long and strong for the first time in my life; and my hair grows faster. And, I feel better. See if your doctor thinks you can benefit from vitamins, too.

CHANGE YOUR STYLE

Study the man or woman just ahead of you on the escalator. Look at the details of the way the person cares for himself/herself. Look at accessories—briefcase, handbag, shoes, the condition of the shoes, hands, nails, rings, jewelry, scarves.

Study the smooth, polished look of a woman's makeup, cut and style of hair. Watch the way the person carries himself/herself, the way the person walks.

Watch the person's manner of handling others whom he or she may say something to.

Soon you'll begin to notice such differences of detail that you'll realize you have sensitized your awareness like radar and can automatically recognize the Rich anytime, anywhere.

Once you do, you'll begin to gradually change yourself to look more the way they do in the detail of self-care. And, it's important that you do.

Why? Because birds of a feather *do* flock together. And the way they recognize each other is by their feather. So you have to take on the feather of the Rich as much as you can without being pretentious.

You don't pretend you are Rich to them. You simply look and behave *as* one of them so they realize you are elevatable.

The Rich who are looking for a mate will not care as much that you don't have money; but that you are elevatable— able to fit in, to become one of them with ease, or, if not one of them, at least to be yourself comfortably among them. That's not snobbish. It's being considerate.

CHANGE THE WAY YOU DRESS

You can identify a priest by his clothing. You can identify a police officer, or a businessperson by clothing.

Clothing identifies who you are in your world.

If you met someone who was dressed and groomed in such a manner that you could not relate to them, you would never know if the person had a heart of gold or not.

Being dressed the way the RMs are dressed makes you immediately identifiable and related to. Even if you are poor, if you are appropriate to an RM's taste, you are elevatable. You can *learn* to be elevatable. Dress the part.

For Men

1. The book, *Man at His Best: Esquire's Guide to Style*, is a good reference work for you.

2. Men can also pick up brochures and leaflets in fine

men's stores or men's sections of the best department stores and study the clothing. Also, study the clothing in good men's fashion magazines, such as *GQ* and *Esquire*.

You don't have to look as extreme in your clothing as some of the clothes the male models wear; but it will keep you aware of trends in styles for:

(a) hair length
(b) facial hair
(c) sideburn length
(d) lapel width
(e) tie width
(f) accessories
(g) fabrics
(h) pattern combinations for the upcoming seasons

You can alter yourself accordingly.

3. Keep your nails short.

4. As for jewelry, men need one really good watch. I was told that Tiffany's advises gentlemen not to wear diamonds.

Excellent pieces of jewelry can be bought secondhand, sometimes from pawn shops and gold and silver exchanges.

The economy in the last few years has had many well-to-do families quietly selling off their jewelry. You could come up with a real find.

5. Wear a vibrant tie or an unusual tie. Neiman-Marcus had a tie with the Statue of Liberty on it that I thought was fabulous! It can be a conversation starter.

6. You may want to put a handkerchief that matches your tie in your jacket pocket.

For Women

1. Choose sophisticated, body-conscious clothing in vibrant colors. Some of the body-conscious clothing I like are classic styles of Ellen Tracy silks.

2. Wear bright gold jewelry near your face and on your wrists.

3. Have a few preppy styles.

4. The shorter French manicure is currently in style. You can give yourself an inexpensive and very good one with Sally Hanson's French manicure kit that you buy at the supermarket.

5. For longer nail styles, I like Lee press-on nails for an emergency. Salons today offer reasonable prices for long and short nails. Check into them.

6. Do try to have one piece of really good, unusual jewelry that is a conversation starter.

7. Have some good, reasonably priced costume jewelry as well.

8. Have a professional makeup make-over by a professional makeup artist, not a cosmetic salesperson. The salesperson will do the best for you he can; but he has to sell the cosmetics he represents.

A professional makeup artist will look at your cosmetics first, show you how to apply them in such a way as to resculpt your features (ask for a glamour look), and tell you what is best for you.

Many wealthy women have professional makeup artists come to their houses to resculpt them with makeup before they go somewhere special. The same is true for their debutante daughters.

I suggest you have a professional makeup make-over every two years to keep up with makeup changes and the changes in your skin texture, coloring, etcetera.

For Both Men and Women

1. Color-charting can make the biggest difference of all as to whether or not you show up well in your clothing.

People often make the mistake of thinking that color-charting means there are colors you should not wear.

Nothing could be further from the truth!

Color charting lets you wear beautifully every single color there is by making sure that you wear the *right shade of every color*! Very important!

In my own case, there are some shades of red that make me look like mud; whereas the right shade of red on me makes me look great, no matter what. Get color-charted and use your correct color shades and tints.

2. Good resale shops can help you dress up your feather with designer clothing in good, quality merchandise. Some wealthy people do this themselves.

Do buy new clothing for the most part, though. The resale items should just be to flesh out a few sparse areas of your wardrobe and to fill it with good accessories at half the price.

3. Pure fabrics are "Richer" looking. Linens, wools, cottons, silks. Also, knits, cashmere, suedes and various leathers are Rich-looking. There are some man-made fabrics that are okay to wear; but have mostly the purer ones.

4. Wear an excellent fragrance that makes you feel expensive and exciting.

5. Have your teeth as white as possible. See a cosmetic dentist and inquire about the fabulous new services available at reasonable prices that can whiten your teeth beautifully. Also, there are procedures that are painless, fast, and cost-effective for correcting dental defects. Beautiful teeth can take you a long way.

6. Have a yummy breath. Rely on hygiene, not mints.

7. Carry an inexpensive clothes brush in the glove compartment of your car to brush off lint or loose threads.

8. Keep a hanger in the back seat and hang up your jackets when you drive so you don't look rumpled.

9. Check clothing seams for loose threads.

10. Keep a cloth under your car seat to wipe a shine onto your shoes.

11. If you're really poor, as I was, buy a can of spray at the shoe store that matches your shoes to keep them looking new when they start looking beaten. Read instructions

carefully and use in a well-ventilated area, not breathing fumes.

12. If you need shoes in a different color, buy a can of spray in that color and spray-paint your shoes to match your outfit.

13. No rings on your left hand.

14. If there is a feature that bothers you, talk to several board-certified plastic surgeons who *specialize* in your area of interest. Talk to people who have had the surgery you desire by the surgeons you are considering, so you can see the results and have your questions answered.

15. Remember, you can tell, just by looking at someone who is dressed for a social occasion, how that person feels about the opposite sex, about themselves, and about sex itself.

If you don't believe me, just look at the covers of single women's and men's magazines sometime. They dress their cover models to send a message that is loud and clear to the opposite sex that they are packaged for relationships.

You want everything about you to say that you believe . . .

1. The opposite sex is wonderful.
2. You are wonderful.
3. Sex is wonderful.

Changing your feather changes your life. It's fun and it gets results.

HAVE A ROLE MODEL IF IT HELPS

You don't want to clone anybody! However, having a role model is part of the learning process. It's like going by a recipe when you're learning to cook. Later, you can add ingredients to individualize, but for the time being, it's the way you learn your basics.

Role models were indispensable for me. I've had many at different times in my life. Some of them include:

Cinderella
Dale Evans (age 5)
My good friend's mother
My aunt Grace
Helen Gurley Brown
Dr. Joyce Brothers
Queen Esther of the Old Testament
Fictional Emma Hart in *A Woman of Substance* by
    Barbara Taylor Bradford
The mistress of a man I admired
Several men I dated
Barbara Sher, author of *Wishcraft*
My daughter
Me (my own potential. It took awhile to get to this point
    and I evolved through all of the above.)

5

Having Class and Good Manners

You don't want to be perfect. If you're too perfect, you lose the magnetism of your own special charm.

—GINIE POLO SAYLES

People often ask me to define "class." The expression *class* refers to behavior and self-care that distinguishes a person as being from the upper social class.

Preceding chapters have dealt with class in terms of self-care. This chapter deals with class in terms of behavior.

Class is the art of making others comfortable. All good manners are built out of the intention to be considerate of the feelings of someone else. Tact, diplomacy, tolerance are all part of the qualities you express. You express humor, but never ridicule.

Approach people with appreciation for their differences, with appreciation for their distinctive traditions.

Personally, I think it's best not to make reference to class at all in conversation. You could accidentally step on your own toes.

Changing your feather into a finer class includes learning basic good manners. Keep in mind as you learn this that you never, never, never want to be *too perfect* in your behavior because it looks too prim, fake, and self-conscious. *Practice* when you're alone and in front of a mirror until it feels natural to you.

Then, put it on automatic when you go out. Concentrate on projecting warmth and joy, not on worrying about whether or not you're doing the right thing. By concentrating on projecting a sparkling personality, your practice sessions will pay off in spontaneous behavior. You won't be self-conscious.

A few guidelines on etiquette follow. If it seems to you that women are being treated as if helpless, dismiss that from your mind. The truth is, etiquette is designed to present an orderly way of doing things. One person is designated to lead the occasion simply because if there are two or more people and they all try to open a door at the same time, or all begin talking to the waiter at the same time, confusion reigns. Knowing a specific procedure is efficient for everyone.

Designations of procedure by sex create an immediate knowledge of what you are to do in a situation to make it flow more smoothly.

Bearing that in mind, you will want to know the following guidelines:

ENTERING OR LEAVING A LIMOUSINE OR AUTOMOBILE

Men: You enter a car after a woman or women. You get out of the car first and offer a hand to each woman inside, one at a time, to help her alight from the car more easily.

Women: Allow the door to be opened for you. This is not a sign of helplessness; it is considerate of the fact that women often have handbags, sometimes fuller skirts to smooth as they get inside, coats on their arms, etcetera.

Don't enter a car headfirst, bending into it. Don't straddle one foot in, followed by the other foot.

Instead, when the door is opened for you, stand close to the opening. Keep both feet together on the ground.

Angle your body sideways, almost with your back to the car interior. Bend both knees, and enter, fanny first, onto the car seat, followed by your upper torso and head.

Your legs and feet will still be outside the car although the rest of your body will be inside the car.

Keep your knees together and your feet together while you lift them into the car.

To exit: Wait for your driver or escort to open your door. Extend your hand outside the open car door for the waiting driver or escort to take.

Knees together and feet together, put both feet on the ground. Lean slightly onto your escort's hand for support, and lift yourself out.

HOW TO ARRIVE AT AND LEAVE A HOSTED EVENT

Men and Women: If you are invited to a private event, find out the names of the host and hostess from your RM. Or if your RM is attending with you, then be sure you supply their names in advance and tell a little about them.

If someone other than the host or hostess answers the door, give your name immediately and state the event you are there to attend. Have your invitation in hand if the event requires it.

Go first to the host and/or hostess if they are not at the door and offer your greetings. They will be near the door if they don't answer it.

Make your remarks to the host and hostess a light, breezy bit of small talk—only seconds—and introduce your RM or be introduced by your RM, if you are with a date.

Don't linger or open a full-fledged conversation because they have other guests arriving.

Usually, they will indicate where you are to go next. As soon as they do, go. In some cases, they may lead you to a group or person and deposit you there to get you involved in the event so they can return to their welcoming task.

At the end of the event, do not leave without seeking out your host and/or hostess and complimenting with something specific about the event and their having given it. Thank them and then leave.

INTRODUCTIONS

Learn to make introductions effortlessly.

Women and Men: If you are introducing a man to a woman, say the name of the woman first, and look at her—''Jane, I'd like you to meet (glance at the man)—John Doe.'' Then, looking at John, say, ''John, this is Jane Smith.'' Look back at Jane. Look at people as you say their names.

If the man is of special prominence—a mayor, senator, a gentleman of great age, or if it is an employer to a new employee—then you will state his name first, using his title if he has one—Mayor Doe, may I present Jane Smith.''

Whenever you are introduced, there are many acceptable responses; but the one considered always appropriate is, ''How do you do.'' If you practice it a few times, you can rattle it off with ease and not sound the least bit pretentious.

Also, learn to introduce yourself with ease by looking a person in the eyes with an expression of pleasure and say in a forthright voice, ''I'm Ginie Polo Sayles. What is your name?''

If you want to extend your hand, do so in a direct manner. For informal occasions, you seem especially warm if you fold your other hand on top of theirs in a double clasp during the handshake.

Men: You always stand for an introduction. You shake hands with any man introduced and with a woman who has offered her hand first.

HANDLING AN EMBARRASSING MOMENT

Men and Women: The way to handle an embarrassing moment is to make as little of it as possible. Play down your mistake and the mistakes of others. Ignore whatever you did or didn't do and force your mind onto something else. Go on smoothly.

RESTAURANTS

Learn to handle yourself in fine restaurants, and at dinner.

Men: Be sure your date likes a particular type of food or the restaurant where you will be taking her. Telephone the restaurant and make reservations, specifying a particular table at that time if you can. Give the date, time, your last name, and how many people will be with you.

Men: Open the door for your date, then stand out of the way to let her pass through the doorway first.

If you wear a hat, remove it as you enter. Men are never to wear a hat inside a building.

Help your date remove her coat. Find out where it is to be checked or carry it for her. Give your name to the host, hostess, or to the headwaiter/maitre d'hotel (commonly referred to as the maitre d'). State the number of guests you have with you, and confirm the time of your reservations.

If you have a seating preference, put a nice tip in the palm of your hand. Place it in the headwaiter's hand in a handshake as you make your seating request.

Do not make your tip excessive; just nice, according to the caliber of restaurant. Anywhere from $10 to $30 is probably good for most places.

The headwaiter controls the dining room and will probably see to it that you are placed with the waiter of top service. Plus, the headwaiter will likely remember you the next time you dine there.

Women: Let your date take your coat, once inside a restaurant.

You follow the restaurant host, hostess, or the maitre d'hotel through the restaurant to the table. Your date follows you. If, for some reason, the headwaiter does not lead you, then you follow your date to the table.

Stand to the left of your chair and allow the headwaiter or your date to pull out your chair for you.

Sit down briefly on the edge of the chair and then lift

slightly. The headwaiter or your date will scoot the chair under you toward the table.

Your date sits to your left.

Men: Seat your date to your right. If there is another woman having dinner with you and your date and she is unescorted, you seat her as well.

You never sit down until every woman in your group is seated.

Men and Women: The minute you are seated, immediately pick up your napkin and unfold it across your lap. Sometimes the headwaiter will do this for you; but don't wait for him to do so.

Women: To avoid confusion, one person commands the dinner. In most cases, that is your date.

Do not order for yourself. Tell your order to your date before the waiter returns. If, however, the waiter returns before you do so, give your order to your date, looking at your date, not at the waiter.

If, during the meal, there is anything you want, tell your date and let him summon the waiter and order it.

Men and Women: Many fine restaurants do not have prices on the woman's menu. For a woman, don't ask about it. Simply order what you want. For a man, you can set the price tone by suggesting a particular item or mentioning that it is your choice.

Course Order

A formal meal may have five courses that are served in this order:

first course: soup/fruit/seafood cocktail
second course: fish
third course: meat
fourth course: salad
fifth course: dessert

Variations in these courses are more typical, but you want to know that the order in which they are listed above is correct.

Silverware

Frequently, the appropriate silver is presented for the course being served and unnecessary silver is removed.

If not, remember that silverware is used in order beginning with the utensil farthest away from either side of your plate and progressing in toward your plate.

Soup

Sip soup from the side of your spoon and place your spoon on the serving plate when you pause while eating and when finished.

Beverages

Use your napkin every time before drinking anything.

Bread and Butter

There are no butter plates used in a formal dinner. Instead, use your upper left side of your plate for butter or bread.

To butter bread, break off a teeny, tiny piece of bread and hold it with one hand, while buttering the teeny piece. Replace your knife, and eat the entire teeny piece in one bite. Never butter a large piece of bread.

Eating

Taste your food before salting it.

You may choose your eating style from either the Continental or the American style. Both are proper.

The Continental Style

The Continental style of eating is done by holding your fork—prongs down—in your left hand and simultaneously holding your knife—cutting blade down—in your right hand—both held over your plate.

Anchor meat with your fork and then cut. After you have cut one bite of meat from the serving on your plate, you immediately lift your fork, which is still in your left hand—prongs down with meat on it—to your mouth and eat it, continuing to hold your knife in your right hand.

You also hold both fork and knife in the position described, waiting, while you chew and swallow your food. Then you proceed into cutting your next bite.

If you rest during the meal, cross your fork—prongs down—on the bottom left, angling over your knife to the right bottom, forming an X.

The American Style

The American style of eating begins the same as the Continental style for cutting meat. Once the meat is cut and is on the fork prongs, you put your knife across the top of your plate—cutting side toward the center of the plate.

Shift your fork from your left hand to your right hand, turning the prongs upward (with the meat still on the prongs) in the process.

Rest your left hand in your lap, lift your fork to your mouth to take the food. Place your fork in the center of your plate and rest both hands in your lap while you chew.

Once you have swallowed your food, you then cross your left hand over your plate to pick up your fork and begin the process again.

Which Style?

Both styles are equally correct. Say nothing about a person's Continental or American eating style preference.

Interruptions at the Table

Women: Before you leave the table during a meal, tell your date so he will stand and come to your chair. If you tell him and he does not do so, then, of course, handle it yourself.

Men: If your date indicates she wants to leave the table during the meal, you stand if she is in the process of rising when she tells you.

If she says so while seated, stand and come to her chair, pulling it out for her. Go back to your chair when she walks away.

When she returns, stand and again seat her. If for some reason she arrives at her chair and begins seating herself before you see her, stand and remain standing until she is seated. Then sit down.

Standing for your date to rise or to be seated is always in order if she leaves the table during the meal. As to whether or not you help her with her chair depends on your reasonable accessibility to her seating.

Men and Women: Whenever you leave the table during a meal, put your napkin on the table, not on your chair. Replace it in your lap immediately when you return.

Men: If an acquaintance approaches your table, always stand, placing your napkin casually to the left of your plate.

Greet your acquaintance and shake hands if convenient. Immediately and briefly introduce your acquaintance to your date and then to anyone else at the table.

Remain standing until your acquaintance leaves your table. Reseat yourself, replacing your napkin in your lap.

Women: Remain seated, but stop eating, if an acquaintance approaches your table. If the acquaintance is someone you know but that your date does not know, immediately introduce them. When the person leaves and your date is reseated, resume eating.

Finger Bowls and Dessert

Men and Women: Finger bowls are served on a doily in your dessert plate. It will be placed in front of you, where your plate belongs. You pick up the finger bowl and doily together and move them to the left of the plate it is on. Your dessert silver will be on the plate also.

Dessert is most often eaten with a spoon. The dessert fork accompanying the spoon is used to anchor the dessert as you cut it with your spoon.

After dessert, dip your fingers only into your finger bowl and dry them on your napkin. Try not to call attention to doing this.

Leaving the Restaurant

Women: When it is time to leave, your date will return behind your chair. Slightly lift your body and he will pull the chair back somewhat so that when you sit again, you are on the edge. Then lift, and as he pulls the chair again, you stand. Some men offer one hand to a woman just before she stands.

As you stand to leave, place your napkin casually to the left of your plate.

Follow your date out of the restaurant dining room.

Allow your date to hold your coat open for you to slip into. If he doesn't do so automatically, then ask him to hold it open for you.

Men: Hold your date's coat open for her to slip into more easily.

SHOULD YOU TRY TO MEET OTHER RMS WHEN YOU ARE ON A DATE WITH ONE?

Absolutely! Your date tonight may not be your date next month or even next week. Don't be loyal to someone you may never see again.

If your date is buying your dinner, keep your perspective. He or she is buying your dinner, not your loyalty. The place where you are is an excellent opportunity to meet RMs— *plus*—you, male or female, are more desirable to other RMs when you are with a date.

Even if you are dating fairly regularly, as long as you are not married, use every opportunity to cultivate more RMs.

Therefore, for both men and women, anytime you are with a date in an expensive restaurant, be attentive to your date. At the same time, be aware of who else is there. Excuse yourself at least once during the evening for the restroom or a telephone call.

Once you are out of your date's view, flirt and start conversations with others who appear to be clearly well-heeled. Have a few personal cards with you in a pocket or bag that you can give someone. Ask for theirs. Follow up.

COCKTAIL AND OTHER PARTIES

Getting drunk is not a good idea. American author F. Scott Fitzgerald married a girl of affluence, but he was never able to fit in with her social set because he couldn't handle alcohol.

Everyone has a few bad moments in life, but more than that can put a question mark on your social reputation.

HANDLING SOCIAL DIFFERENCES

Politely honor a person's no-smoking preference, no matter how you feel about it.

And don't be the one to tell crude jokes or to use profanity in a social situation, even if others do.

Although we all know social classes exist, it's best to not refer to social classes at all. I don't care who else does, just don't. You could accidentally step on your own toes.

EXPRESSING OPINIONS AT A SOCIAL EVENT

A social event is held for pleasure and very light mental stimulation with interesting companions.

That means it's okay to express an opinion that is different from someone else's—occasionally. The main thing to keep in mind is that this is a *social* occasion and not a legal debate.

I would have to say that more people ostracize themselves from friendships and society for this one major breach of social etiquette than for any other.

No one will remember who was right or wrong in an opinion, but they will remember who was rude or pushy or hostile and will avoid that person.

Refrain from being aggressively opinionated—even if the hair is rising on the back of your neck at what someone else is saying. In such cases, it's best not to say anything, but to move to another group that is talking pleasantly.

In cases where opinions are being stated with friendly differences, you can pleasantly state your position, and stick to it; but be tolerant. Be gracious in social settings.

And, although you and I are having straight talk here, it's a little bit tacky to take on too much about money or possessions.

BUILDING CONVERSATIONAL RAPPORT

If you want someone to feel instant rapport with you, just listen closely while the person tells you something.

Then, simply give a *summary* of what the person just told you and say it back to the person, beginning with, "Oh, I see, you mean that . . ."

This is almost magic! It can certainly make you seem charming to an RM's friends and to your RM. You seem to really understand.

FINAL TIDBITS

Men lead the way down the stairs (women often wear high-heeled shoes that can easily catch; he blocks her fall). At the foot of the stairs, he turns and extends his hand to her. She takes his hand as she descends the last few steps.

Men follow a woman up the stairs (again, in case he is needed to block her fall).

Men also lead the way into dark areas, such as a theater.

He walks behind her if an usher leads into a dark area.

Applaud by clapping one hand into the other hand, that is cupped and still.

Gum-chewing in public is taboo for both men and women.

6

Body-Flirting

> Everything we do is a learned skill. Skills give you more control over your life. Skills are your best friend.
>
> —GINIE POLO SAYLES

"Maybe . . ."

Your most effective flirting signal says, "Maybe . . ."

You're not saying yes, and you're not saying no. You're signaling maybe . . .

Maybe is sexier than either yes or no.

Maybe is sexy flirting. And flirting is the last safe sex we have, so enjoy it to the full!

Flirting is a fabulous skill for interacting with RMs. Flirting allows you to send up trial balloons before risking a more serious investment of time and interest.

You don't just flirt with your eyes. You flirt with your body, through the body language of clothing and your posture. You signal your attitude with your facial expression—especially your eyes and the energy in your face.

BODY FLIRTING AND CLOTHES

For men, clothing guidelines are given in Chapter 4.

For women, I recommend a sophisticated, body-conscious clothing style over the preppy look.

Preppy has evolved to an ageless, timeless dress style of nothing too low-cut or showy. And it's a quality, nice look.

However, a women's fashion magazine polled men nationwide a few years back and found that most men consider preppy styles too plain and boring.

Men like it occasionally as a change but not daily as an ongoing look. A sophisticated look was the look that won.

Preppy clothing is mainly part of the body language among women who are married or who don't have to establish themselves with an appearance that has instant impact.

Preppy clothing says "I'm not a threat. I'm sexless and safe. I'm a woman's woman."

Sophisticated body-conscious clothing says, "I am a threat. I like men, sex, and me. I'm serious about relationships and if you don't take care of your man, I'll get him."

Do have some preppy clothing to wear when you're with other women and occasionally with men for the subtle impact of the preppy style; but sophisticated body-conscious clothing in vibrant colors attracts Rich Men as long as the clothes are tasteful.

THE BODY-FLIRTING OF POSTURE

When a man is available, he sits or stands in a full-front, open position (no crossed arms or feet or legs), facing the main action in the situation. He looks women over, even if discreetly. He looks longer at a woman he is interested in than a woman would look at a man she is interested in. He arranges proximity to a woman he wants to meet or to groups of women in general.

When a woman is sensuously available for a relationship, she sits with one leg crossed over the other *and* the higher her leg is crossed on her other thigh, the higher wattage her signal is!

Crossing her leg this way forces a provocative arch at the base of her spine, jutting her breasts up and forward. Very mating-callish.

If she crosses her leg down low over her other knee, she is simply resting. The more interested in men she gets, the higher her crossed leg mounts!

Posture is integral to sexy flirting. Try flirting with slumped shoulders. Just try it!

VERBAL FLIRTING

You can speak or not because flirting can be either verbal or nonverbal.

The most important thing to know is that it doesn't matter what you say. Just say something. You don't have to say anything clever, intelligent, or even half-bright—just say something. You make simple, forgettable comments.

An RM seldom remembers what you've said, only that a connection was made between you that allows him/her to interact with you now.

My husband and I can't remember what our first conversation was about. It doesn't matter—we're married.

THE IMPORTANCE OF SKILLS

Success with RMs is more likely according to your proficiency in the signals you send for courtship behavior and relationship skills.

At one time, I would have turned my nose up at the notion that a person needs skills to meet and marry an RM.

Skills. The word had a phony ring to me. It sounded as if I would have to play-act or pretend to be something I wasn't.

I felt that if he were the right one, or meant to be, that I wouldn't have to do anything at all. No indeed, I thought that all behavior would fall into place *naturally* with that person.

Then I began to realize that just because you have all the right ingredients in your kitchen, doesn't mean you know how to cook. And, there is no disgrace in learning the skills from a cookbook.

Skills are your very best friend. Skills are the nicest thing you can give yourself—because skills give you greater control over your own life. And that includes your social life, your relationship life.

THE SKILL OF FLIRTING

Flirting succeeds best when you are in a fun or light-hearted frame of mind—energy high. You can't flirt successfully when you're depressed or tired.

I had to train myself to "rev up" and flirt. The following is the rev-up formula I used successfully and that many of my students have found works.

1. Deliberately arch your back into the highest, best posture of anyone.
2. Deliberately walk at a much quicker pace as part of the rev up.
3. As you walk, begin to concentrate on liking everything around you so that your face and eyes take on a lively sense of excitement (excitement stimulates love gland responses).

That's how I revved up. If you use my technique, then as you are walking with a frisky purpose somewhere and your posture is provocatively high and your face is luminous, happy, you look deliberately into the eyes of *every* man you pass for 2 full, piercing seconds—and then slide your eyes away to the direction you're walking.

At the moment your eyes begin sliding away, start smiling. You are now smiling after the fact, not during the eye contact—although you looked radiantly happy as you entered eye contact.

You can actually count 2 full seconds of flirting eye contact if you like. In flirting, 1—2—glide your eyes away!

Don't jerk your eyes away because that looks fearful or as if you didn't like the person.

If you have positioned yourself where RMs are (see Chapter 7), you'll have turned at least a few Rich heads, even though some probably won't respond at all—that's how it is for all of us, so don't worry about it.

THE IMPORTANCE OF PRACTICE

But the instant you do get a negative response, then you must do it again with someone else, and someone else, and someone else until you get the response you're looking for.

Practice means "it doesn't count." So if you get a negative response from someone, it doesn't count, because you're just practicing.

And when you do get the response you're looking for, do it again and again, logging into your system only the responses that you like—shrugging off the ones you don't like.

SUCCESS IS A NUMBERS GAME

If you are flirting with only 5 people a day and 3 of them—or even 1 of them responds negatively, then you may feel a little rejected.

But, if you are flirting with 25 to 50 people a day and as many as 10 of them don't respond, you won't care! You won't even remember them!

That's why it's so important not to pin all your hopes on the response of one RM—because if it doesn't work, you're defeated.

If, on the other hand, you are open to *all* RMs for flirting and conversation, then you increase your chances with everyone you meet. You have put the odds on your side.

Prepare for the opportunity. Prepare, prepare, prepare. Prepare means to practice your social, flirting, conversation, sparkly, smooth, people skills and you'll be ready for your RM.

For those of you who saw me on *Donahue* with my students who met a Rich man during a fieldtrip, the following checklist is the one they used when it happened.

ASSIGNMENT CHECKLIST

Goal Reinforcement: Casual interaction is the first lesson in flirting. Interact spontaneously with the opposite sex every single day in any of the following ways at three random (and safe) locations.

Locations

1	2	3	
—	—	—	Freshen grooming
—	—	—	Posture (what does your posture tell the world about how you feel?)
—	—	—	Pace (walk just a fraction faster than your usual walk)—not just amble along as if you have no place to go and nothing to do. Move with energy.
—	—	—	Look with interest at the environment around you as you move. Stop occasionally and show interest in something nearby.
—	—	—	Have an "I know you like me" expression; not a "Do you like me?" self-worth questioning expression.
—	—	—	Notice people and smile without lingering—both sexes, all ages.
—	—	—	Be observant of every place as to the number of people of the opposite sex.
—	—	—	Notice traffic patterns in places you go and walk against it/sit facing it/stand at the crossroads of it or at the end of it (1—2—look away!).
—	—	—	Don't overstay in one place or leave too soon.
—	—	—	Make a comment in passing about whatever a person is looking at, in the same friendly tone you would make it to a friend.

___   ___   ___   Every time you interact with someone, congratulate yourself with pride for having done so, *no matter what you said* (as long as it was not crude).

___   ___   ___   Speak first to someone who is standing next to the person you want to meet, so the person can see you interact with others (your friendly personality). Also, it is then nonthreatening when you say something to the person you're interested in.

___   ___   ___   Check center displays, seating areas, stairs, escalators.

___   ___   ___   1—2—look away. Don't jerk your eyes away. Let your eyes *glide* away to the side.

___   ___   ___   If in a restaurant, show quiet but cheerful animation with waiter/waitress. Don't flirt with the waiter/waitress (unless you're interested!).

This allows others to observe your personality in pleasant, general, friendly interaction.

SELF-EVALUATION

Assignment # _____
Assigned Locations:

How many women/men did you see en route to
store #1? _____
store #2? _____
store #3? _____

How many women/men were in:
store #1? _____
store #2? _____
store #3? _____

Where, en route, were you when you made your comments-in-passing? _____

To whom did you make your comments? (general description, if no name) _____

What were the comments you made in passing? _____
_____

How did you tie in your comment to the situation or person? _____
_____

Did you say it nonthreateningly? _____

Did you care what the person's response was? (If so, that inhibits you. Learn to not dwell on what the response is, and make another comment to someone else.) _____

Did you establish eye contact (friendly but not personal, not meaningful)? _____

Did you keep walking? _____

How did you feel *just before or as* you made your comment or question? _____

What was your immediate feeling *after* you said it? _____

What was your self-talk afterward? Did you feel good about it and that whatever you said was all right? _____

Did you feel as if you said something wrong? _____

Did you feel self-conscious? _____

Did you use your body as a ''buffer''? _____

Did you immediately feel exultant that you said something, no matter how you felt before doing so? (You should, because you were successful by achieving your personal goal of interacting.) _____

Did you feel uncomfortable or self-conscious at any time?

_____

If so, at exactly what point each time—and why? _____

_____

What do you consider your biggest problem in this exercise? _____

Realize that *only you* can solve the problem through practicing whatever was uncomfortable for you, over and over, until you are competent in that area of interaction skill. It will not come to you any other way.

Take the area that you felt was your biggest problem and zero in on it as your number-one priority in your next assignment, while continuing to fulfill the rest of the checklist as well.

PART II

Meeting the Rich

7

Where the Rich Are

Class with sass!—That's the personality that succeeds with the Rich.

—GINIE POLO SAYLES

Where do you find RMs?

Let's look at the problem with giving names of exact places. The biggest problem is that it changes. By the time the general populace finds where they are and begins going there, the RMs have switched over to another place.

Often, they are in the places that cost the most to be, which is the second problem, if you have limited funds.

The third problem is that they frequently go places during seasons and hours that most people don't or can't go there.

However, a quick list of some specifics can include:

1. They go where it is warm when the weather is cold and where it is cool when the weather is hot.
2. They can be found at some country clubs, but not just any country club.
3. They are at fine estate auctions.
4. They are at quiet, elegant hotels.
5. They attend opening nights of major performances.
6. They can be found at tennis and golf tournaments.
7. They often conduct business over breakfast, lunch, formal tea—hence the terms power breakfast, power lunch, power tea.
8. They patronize some charity events and socialize at those charity fund-raisers or balls.
9. They are in airports—especially in corporate terminals for private planes.

10. They attend some shareholder meetings.
11. They sit in boxes at football games.
12. They go to yacht clubs.
13. They will be at horse races.
14. They go to high-performance car races.
15. They can easily be found at gambling centers, such as Atlantic City, Las Vegas, Monte Carlo.
16. They frequent high-ticket political events.

Now, if you feel depressed about being able to go to these places to get to them, remember, they are also at work, if they work, and in their neighborhoods, at least some of the time.

Neighborhood and work are the two places they are the most meetable and cost the least for you to be there.

NEIGHBORHOOD

Aristotle Onassis said that if you want to be rich you must live where the rich live—even if it's in an attic—and that you must go where the rich go and do what the rich do.

To live where the Rich live means changing your address—revealed by your zip code, and your telltale telephone prefix.

In real estate, the motto is "Location, location, location." Make that your motto for finding an RM. Location *is* everything.

Find the area of your town where the Rich live and *live there,* period. If it's old, has no dishwasher, no washer-dryer connections, no pool or club house, *still* live there.

Living in their neighborhoods is like having an ear to the ground as to what's in, what's out, where they go, when they go, and all the constant changes they make in their "hangouts." This keeps you current and moving with the flow of both when and where they go.

Equally important, though, is that you will absorb much

of the value system of the Rich by osmosis, just living among them.

Think of yourself as fresh hot water and think of the neighborhood as a fine exotic tea. By combining the two for a period of time—known as "steeping," the water takes on the flavor and color of the tea!

That's exactly how it is, living among the Rich. The flavor and color of their lives steep into you and you become like them—identifiable as one of them.

Plus, you become *visible* to the Rich. They can *see* you. When you buy groceries or dash to a convenience store, it may as well be in the most elusive neighborhood supermarkets or convenience stores.

That's true of anything you have to do in your daily life. Make no mistake about it; it's in your daily-life situations that you are best able to meet people if you make yourself accessible by following the guidelines for confidence in Chapter 3.

Pharmacy, liquor store, card shop, bookstore, bank, automatic teller machines, coffee shops, car washes, cleaners— anything. Wealthy people support the businesses in their neighborhoods and they don't always have the help doing everything for them.

I've seen a man worth $50 million stop by the cleaners to drop off something he had with him, simply because it was on his way. Yes, he had a domestic staff who normally took care of his cleaning. Nevertheless, the Rich do stop to do mundane tasks on occasion—especially in their neighborhoods.

So, even if you live in an attic, you have the neighborhood in common with the Rich.

As we said when we were discussing the importance of being mercenary, you want to accumulate as much in common with the Rich as possible. So:

1. Being mercenary is something you have in common with the Rich.

2. Their neighborhood (zip code, telephone prefix) is something you will then have in common with the Rich.
3. Dressing of their feather is something you will have in common with the Rich.

Living in the neighborhood is important for another reason. In her book, *How To Get Whatever You Want Out of Life*, Dr. Joyce Brothers says that most people marry someone who lives within 16 blocks of them—someone right in their own neighborhoods!

So take a look around at the 16 blocks surrounding you and see if you want to marry someone from your neighborhood—which means that you may spend the rest of your life in that neighborhood or its equivalent.

Get out of your neighborhood into the wealthiest one. Plunk yourself down right in the middle of the nicest 16 blocks surrounding you that you can possibly afford to squeeze yourself into that is closest to the very best.

SHOPPING

Men may be able to meet wealthy women who are shopping. The key here is that wealthy women—and wealthy men—typically do not shop during the weekends and evenings.

Saturdays, Sundays, and weeknights are filled with working-class people who are shopping on their days off or their hours off.

Wealthy people, who control their own hours, choose the less crowded weekday hours when they won't have to mingle with the masses.

They can have more privacy, be around people who are more like themselves, receive better, unrushed attention from workers.

Rich women are inclined to make a social occasion of it, too. They will stop for gourmet coffee or tea, or enjoy lunch in a special shop or restaurant.

RESTAURANTS

The Rich seldom frequent chain restaurants, such as popular chain steak houses or chain seafood restaurants that you see advertised on television.

True, there are some people with a lot of money who go to those places at times; but "The" Rich, for the most part, do not go there.

The Rich frequent one-of-a-kind specialty restaurants. Many of these restaurants are beautiful, elegant, and *very* expensive.

However, they will go to a nondescript little hole-in-the-wall in a questionable part of town for a specialty food preparation instead of to the slick, commercialized chain, that has less quality control than the chains advertise as having.

Interestingly, the chains they may go to once in a while are coffee shops, mainly because they're open 24 hours. They go there in the wee hours a time or two, and then give a fair amount of patronage at other hours.

Private membership restaurants and private membership cocktail clubs are part of their status symbol life-style, where they get the kind of treatment and recognition they feel their money deserves; and where they will be with people of their own ilk.

When you do date an RM who is a member, get the RM to take you there so you may meet other RMs.

That's something you can't get into unless you get a job as a host or hostess there. Usually, a host or hostess is not allowed to come into the club as a date with someone who is a member. But there are other fine clubs they can take you to.

The first time you go to the most expensive restaurants in your city, go for lunch. It's the same food but it costs a lot less and you are familiarizing yourself with the menu and the restaurant. Many RMs frequent these places for lunch also.

Posh restaurants, downtown, surrounded by financial centers or in high-rent office complexes attract RMs for lunch. Remember, the Rich will be where the money is and so financial centers and the surrounding restaurants fare well with their patronage.

Don't accept a table that is next to the kitchen or tucked away where no one can see you. Place a tip in the maitre d's hand as you gently insist on the best.

Leave a very nice tip when you get your check your first time there and you will be seated well after that. You can order salad and tea or mineral water if your bank balance is on a diet!

TEA

Call the most exclusive hotels in your area and ask if they serve afternoon tea.

Afternoon tea is typically served in a parlor-type setting with full tea service of teapot, sugar bowl, creamer filled with milk (you do not put cream in tea; you use milk), or lemon instead of milk.

The tea is a loose tea, not a teabag. Loose tea is measured one teaspoon for each person having tea, plus one teaspoon for the pot. It is then steeped in hot water in the teapot for 3 to 5 minutes for peak flavor. A silver strainer that you place over your cup, when you pour, is part of the tea service.

Tea includes crustless sandwiches with light fillings, scones (biscuits) served with clotted cream (whipped cream, instead of butter), and sometimes a beautiful array of delicious pastries and desserts.

When you find a hotel or restaurant in the expensive parts of town or in the business district that serves afternoon tea, go there some weekday afternoon. If you don't know what to do, simply ask the waiter and don't be embarrassed. It is the job of the waiter to serve the tea and to answer any questions to help you enjoy it. You'll love the gentle pleasure of afternoon tea, and being in a location where you may meet RMs.

HAPPY HOUR AND BARS

Go to Happy Hour at expensive hotels. Go to clubs that are in the best business district of your city. You don't have to drink alcohol. You can have mineral water, coffee, or soft drinks.

If you go to clubs or bars on a regular basis, you lose a little bit of the "special" quality that attracts people to you because you are someone new and different from the "usual" crowd. Too, people start thinking of you as a drinker or a lush.

I suggest you select several elegant bars and rotate days and times that you go to each one, so you keep a fresh quality.

EXCLUSIVE CLUBS

Water and wealth mix—alas, privately. Don't despair. Most rich sailing clubs have professionals on staff.

Professionals are usually allowed to use the facilities to teach nonmembers who take private lessons from them.

This practice is true of tennis clubs, and many country clubs as well. Taking lessons is your entree to these places to be seen by the members.

You are on the property of a posh private club that costs upward from $25,000 or more to join—yet you are here for your $35 lesson. You'll see signs that say "Members Only Beyond This Point."

Naturally, you'll ignore the signs. Usually, nobody ever says anything to you; but just in case they do, you can claim you're not wearing your contact lenses or you just didn't see it, or you are considering becoming a member. Stay confident and openly likable.

The only reason you bother to "get lost" on the property is to meet RMs, so make the time count. Chat with a few people. Just make comments about the day. Get a conversation started. Flirt. Don't linger, and do exchange names and cards.

Warning: Because they stay in shape by teaching, most club pros (female as well as male) have healthy, taut, muscle-clinging, lightly tanned, temptingly gorgeous bodies oozing out all over their short-sleeved shirts and shorts.

They are gregarious, gracious, and easily get you turned on. However, most club pros are not rich (and often married), so you probably won't want to get involved with them, if you're aiming for an RM.

SPORTING EVENTS

Professionals are often allowed to invite students to regattas and tournaments. Always go. Attend every single sporting tournament of the best clubs that you can, such as golf tournaments.

If you can get tickets to the pavilion or clubhouse afterward, that's where a lot of socializing will take place.

If you can't get a ticket, start quiet conversations with people you meet on the course.

There are hospitality tents at the tournaments which are just like going to a bar. If you are a woman, buy one drink, and speak to a man nearby who isn't with a date. He may buy your next drink.

If you are following the players on the course, make quiet talk with a few people of the opposite sex; but watch the golfers.

When you move to the next hole, stand next to someone else. Never seem to be deliberately following anyone, although that's what you're casually doing with several people. Find out if the people you meet are members of the club or if they have special pavilion passes. Either way, that means they go to the club afterward.

Most people are drinking alcohol throughout the tournament, and by the 18th hole, they are congenial enough to let you go in as a guest with them, if you ask. And you do have to be gutsy enough to ask in an innocent way.

As the crowd begins surging toward the party areas, you ask, "Where is everyone going?" When told, say, "Oh, this is my first tournament. I didn't realize there would be something going on afterward. I'd love to go in—let me go with you." Don't sound pushy. Sound lovable.

PRESTIGIOUS ART CLASSES

For men, take art classes from a highly esteemed local artist. It can be chock-full of Rich women, often widows, trying to fill up their lives.

You can find out who the highly esteemed local artists who give classes are by first visiting the museum in your city and asking a curator. Also ask the names of the best art galleries in your city.

Then browse through every one of them, asking the gallery personnel if they know who the best local artists are who also give classes.

Some of them will just give the name of a friend of theirs who gives art classes, so you will want to ask all the galleries and see which names emerge time and again.

However, galleries tend to show certain artists, and you're bound to receive some bias, but still, even if each gallery gives you a different name, that's fine—because you are then going to visit the various art supply stores and ask there.

True, you may receive the names of their most frequent customers; but, overall, from these three sources—your local museum of art, art galleries, and art supply shops—you should have a few names to choose from.

Then, contact the artists, expressing an interest in taking

art classes. Ask if you may visit an art class for about 5
minutes sometime soon to see if it is the type of commitment you will be able to make. Every artist I've ever known
has been willing to allow that. However, they get antsy if
you stay very long, so leave after a few minutes.

You are only there to determine if the people in the
classes are prospects. You'll do that by arriving early before
class and watching the cars arrive, then entering the class
before it starts and pleasantly introducing yourself to those
whose cars or style impressed you as moneyed before you
came in.

Notice wedding rings, although some widows wear them.
Ask if their husbands like art, and a widow will say that her
husband has passed away.

You can also mention your profession by saying that art
is a natural extension of your acting career (or a break from
the work you do on inventions, or you're writing a novel
about an artist . . . et cetera). Then you can casually ask
what she does or if she has a particular career.

If you find several women there without specific occu-
pations, enroll! This can be a mecca for a man if he hits the
right artist.

ALCOHOL AND DRUG REHABILITATION CENTERS

Elizabeth Taylor's highly publicized marriage to Larry
Fortensky was the culmination of a love affair that both
began and blossomed at the Betty Ford Clinic for alcohol
and drug rehabilitation in Palm Springs, California.

Some people wonder what prompted unrich Larry to dry
out in a clinic that caters to the rich and famous. But not me.
I offer him my applause for choosing his rehabilitation
clinic wisely. Besides, who could not love Liz Taylor? If
you must dry out, by all means dry out with affluence.

And even if you are not in need of drying out, telephone
the spiffy alcohol and drug rehabilitation clinics in your area
that are frequented by the Rich and find out what other

kinds of programs they have. They may have weight-control programs, weight-gain programs, adult children of alcoholics programs, or public awareness programs that would bring you into proximity with their moneyed clients—for whatever reason they may be there. However, such programs may be costly.

Sometimes clinics may have introductory seminars that cost much less or may even be free.

And, of course, you can telephone the clinics and find out if they have a volunteer program you can become involved in. This gives you reason to be on the property without the cost of anything more than a uniform, your time, and gas money.

If you have a profession in the medical or a related caring industry, why not up your chances of rich romance in your profession by working in an alcohol or drug rehabilitation clinic that caters to wealthy and famous people?

If you are a writer or a would-be writer, why not write about the rich clinics from a firsthand basis (I can tell this is going to start a new wave of articles on the subject!).

A wealthy chapter of Alcoholics Anonymous will also have a few 100-proof millionaires in need of nurturing, understanding, and a new life. It's more honorable if you are a nondrinker.

Call the center for Alcoholics Anonymous and ask for the chapter nearest the most prestigious zip code.

When you go, go early so you can wait outside and check out the people who arrive—their cars, their feather, et cetera. No one has to give a last name or explain why they are there, so feel free to go in. You may want to come up with a reason, though, in case anyone does happen to ask you. Just give a first name and you can either say that you are interested for personal reasons (true) or that you are doing research (you might have to produce credentials if you suggest that, though).

You'll find the experience interesting and educational. And you won't have to worry about getting to know people.

The people there will give their testimonies and you will know exactly how the problem developed for that person, which gives you a way to be the person's solution.

Now, in other parts of this book, I tell you to be a problem for a person in the relationship. This is the one exception to that advice.

People who are recovering alcoholics need supportiveness. If you can't give that, don't go.

I do my best to teach you to be a real asset to an RM's life while keeping you in control of your fate or position in the relationship. I am presuming that you deserve such control and know how to handle it responsibly.

The way to be an asset in this case is to be supportive in accordance with the guidelines that Alcoholics Anonymous gives. It's a great organization.

Incidentally, it has been shown that sometimes love can actually make a positive recovery difference in the life of an alcoholic.

HORSE RACES

There are several types of horse racing. However, the three you should know are:

> Thoroughbred racing;
> Quarterhorse racing; and
> Harness racing.

Usually the local newspapers in track towns will have tips on which horse they predict to win a race. Pick up the paper, along with a racing form, and study it the night before going to the track.

Each type of race attracts different types of spectators, gamblers, and owners. Whichever type you choose may determine the type of people you meet.

For instance, one of the richest purses for quarterhorse racing is a race in New Mexico. There are a lot of cowboy types of people who go there—with or without money. Although there are a lot of city people there, too, it is identified mostly as a cowboy race. I'd go!

Owners

In any type of horse racing, the owner of the horse usually is the one who has the money, and the owner is often present at races.

Some owners will have both thoroughbreds and quarterhorses; but often you will find they tend to have a distinct following of either thoroughbreds or quarterhorses.

Harness racehorse owners stick pretty much to harness racing.

Owners are often found in the clubhouse. You can get into the clubhouse of racetracks. You don't have to have a reserved table or assigned seating or box seat.

Walk around and get acquainted. Learn about horse racing, though, because it gives you a natural conversational tool and these people are serious about racing.

Sometimes, owners sit in the director's private rooms where they place bets and congregate. You can't get in there, but find out if there is one at the track and where it is. Then, keep your eyes open to see who goes in and out and be as near as possible, finding something to say in passing.

It will state in the program who the owners and trainers are. Most of the owners will stay at the race unless it's toward the end.

Let's say you see the first race. Watch who goes down to the winner's circle for the photograph or award, and then observe those people as they come back into the clubhouse. Get close. Create a reason to say something. Watch an owner or trainer and see who they talk to because those are probably horse people, too, who are pretty good-sized bettors with money. These are people to meet.

Types of Owners

There is a different breed of owner for each breed of horse racing. In thoroughbred races, you'll have more owners who hire trainers than you will trainer-owners. A lot of trainer-owners will be at the smaller tracks.

In quarterhorse racing, you have a mixed bag in the sense that there are those owners who hire trainers; then there are some trainer-owners; and there are big guys and small guys, financially.

Those owners whose horses are in the Feature Races—which are the bigger deals—are usually going to be the "bigger guys."

Harness race owners may do it all—own, train, and ride in the race.

Gamblers

In every type of race there will be gamblers from every socioeconomic level placing bets. On a day-in, day-out basis, though, you'll usually find more RMs and celebrities placing bets at thoroughbred tracks than at other types.

Harness racing is often held in the evening and attended as a social event. Social gamblers might take a date to a harness race instead of to the theater.

Each track has its racing season and racing days. Attend every type of race, observe RMs and see which ones you want to pursue.

GAMBLING CENTERS

RMs are frequently found in gambling centers. It's easier to meet someone in a gambling situation that has interaction among the gamblers. Interactive gambling means that people can move in and out of the gambling crowd easily and can interact with each other.

Dice tables (shooting craps) are very popular with large gamblers.

There is a lot of emotion at a dice table. Emotion means excitement, and people fall in love (and get turned on) more during excitement than at any other time. Probably the dice tables are the best places for high interaction.

Some of the games are isolated or don't create much of a social interaction energy.

There are gamblers at blackjack tables; but you don't have as much opportunity to talk to them at a blackjack table.

Baccarat is normally too isolated unless you are a baccarat player yourself.

Roulette can be good but it is more staid, normally with a quieter crowd. However, I like it.

In poker, nobody talks to anybody much.

Slot-machine players are involved with their isolation device—the machine. This is one-on-one. Only a win can generate much interaction.

POLO CLUBS

Telephone polo clubs in your area and have them send you information about attending their events.

Polo players follow the warm seasons. During the winter, they play in California and Florida.

Wealthy women follow this sport quite a bit; however, each club is a personality unto itself. Some polo clubs are society-oriented; some polo clubs are family-oriented.

Wealthy members may be in private boxes; however, there may not be enough private boxes for everyone, so there may be some moneyed members in the grandstands.

VISIBILITY

Learn the art of high visibility. How many movie stars and stage stars do you know of who married money? That's right: virtually all of them. People who position themselves to be seen get to meet RMs.

Star in community theaters, enter pageants, competitive sports, talent contests, any competitive event—and be good enough to get noticed! The Rich like, love, and respect high achievers in virtually any category. Be one.

When you can finally afford it, hire a press agent to promote you and get your name in all the right columns, on all the right invitations.

A woman once told me it was the smartest move she ever made. It helped her end up in the social register.

PUT THE ODDS ON YOUR SIDE

The Bureau of Census is published annually by the government and is available free at your library. Consult it to determine the cities that have the greatest numbers of millionaires, and of singles of the sex opposite yours.

Check it out and decide if you can just as easily do what you are doing in the area with the greatest number of single, opposite-sex millionaires. You can visit during vacation, and if it seems ripe for the picking, locate a job, live there a year at least, and know you have the odds on your side.

And whereas you may very well walk into a small town and pick up the only single millionaire living there, the chances are greater of your meeting and marrying the Rich in a city.

However, being a small-town girl from West Texas, I do know that in its heyday, Midland, Texas, only 30 miles west of my hometown, was so full of millionaires per capita that it was almost impossible for a girl to not date a millionaire at some point! Seriously! So, if you want a small town, at least be sure the statistics bear it out as high in millionaire residents.

ETHNIC RMS

There are people who contact me wanting to meet someone Rich in a particular ethnic category.

To do so, find the progressive cities with the most concentrated population in that ethnic category. You can locate it through the Bureau of Census, published by the government and available at your library. I emphasize a progressive city because you are looking for people who have found a way to be financially successful.

The second thing to do is to get involved with organizations that deal with the business people of that ethnic group. This may include advisory boards for business funding or business management. The advisory boards are generally made up of people with a particular ethnic background who are leaders and who are financially successful.

You should be able to find these organizations through your Better Business Bureau, Chamber of Commerce, or Junior Chamber of Commerce (Jaycees).

Some community college student service centers can direct you to special organizations that network with local ethnic business owners. And, in fact, government-funding agencies may be able to tell you how to get in touch with them.

Local ethnic newspapers and magazines, as well as national ethnic newspapers and magazines, such as *Ebony/Jett,* that targets African-Americans, may be able to provide information on organizations you seek. Write or telephone them. Notice the organizations and events they cover.

Once you have located your area of operation for ethnic RMs, find the nicer clubs and restaurants and neighborhoods in the ethnic communities and join the organizations that are frequented by those who have been successful.

Then, follow all the rest of the advice in this book, because there really is no difference.

8

Jobs to Meet the Rich

Even if you do earn Riches on your own, there is still the problem of finding a mate who shares your monetary values. It is efficient to resolve your romantic and your financial needs in one contract—marriage.

—Ginie Polo Sayles

Yes, there are jobs that let you get paid to meet the Rich—legitimate ones!

JOURNALISM

Journalism is one of the best—you can always stage an interview for a story with an RM of tremendous power. You may even end up sharing the limelight of the RM's power. Our country has had a First Lady who was previously in journalism—Jackie Bouvier Kennedy—later Jackie Onassis.

WORK FOR THE RICH

For women, working for Rich men can be an inside track to learning how to relate to other Rich men. And you are also meeting his wealthy friends.

It's no secret that throughout contemporary history, Rich men, when they have strayed, have strayed mostly with women they met working for their own companies or for companies of people they did business with.

Even if you don't date the Rich men you work for, you

85

learn how they think, what's important to them, the types of people they respond to and those they don't.

You learn how they look in style and grooming. You learn their haunts—where they go, when they go there, and the style in which they go there.

You also—and this is important—get a glimpse of how their wives or girlfriends dress and behave and where these women shop as well as places they frequent in their spare time.

GLAMOUR JOBS

Male glamour jobs include television commercial actors, special fund-raisers for big community projects, handling expensive art auctions, stage or film actors, athletes, community television personalities—weather, sports, news, talk shows.

Glamour jobs for men can also include writers, sculptors, inventors.

High publicity positions can include directorship positions for nonprofit arts organizations, theaters. Usually these positions are not that well-salaried, but the women you can meet who are dedicated patrons are often quite, quite wealthy.

If you are willing to settle for an affair, you and your company can benefit. If you want marriage, you can usually find someone in the ranks who does.

Vows of poverty aside, single ministers and Episcopal priests can easily slip beyond the role of comforter into husband to wealthy widows.

Glamour jobs for women include modeling and stage or film acting or television commercials.

Singers, dancers, performers of any type have an element of glamour. The glamour grows as their publicity grows. The Rich are publicity hounds, although they pretend they aren't.

GLAMOUR-RELATED JOBS

Hostess jobs in fine restaurants and clubs rate well for women to meet RMs, as do some airline jobs. However, the airline pace, demands, and some routes may not be as conducive as you might think. Also, the requirements of being away at odd hours and times can put a strain on the development of relationships.

FINANCE-RELATED JOBS

Clearly, the Rich will be wherever money is—and the center for money and American industry is the stock market. Therefore, jobs in stockbrokerage firms, commodity firms, real estate, some banks, some insurance, and other financial institutions attract the rich.

I unashamedly admit that the deciding factor to becoming a stockbroker was to meet wealthy men. Wealthy men have to do something responsible with their money if they want to stay wealthy, so they seek investments. Too, the profile of wealthy men shows that many of them are gamblers at heart and carry that over into investing in options.

Jobs related to investment give both women and men a legitimate excuse to telephone someone wealthy out of the blue—which is known as a cold call—to introduce yourself, and to suggest getting together for financial planning.

For men, it's best not to actually "work for" a Rich woman as such, unless she is the corporate executive/entrepreneur type.

Your best bet *is* cold-calling for financial institutions and following up with a visit. Your second-best bet is to be in a line of work similar to but a little different from that of her former husband or her father.

She probably has unresolved feelings for those two men and she can transfer them onto you, trying to work out that previous relationship satisfactorily. You will, of course, let her do that—*most* of the time.

PATRON-SUPPORTED JOBS

Men can pretend to be the undiscovered artist, actor, writer, genius, or scientist—someone who is a natural extension of her own social interests. She wants to be a patron. It fulfills a mothering role for her. *Be* her protégé.

EXCLUSIVE CLUBS OR PRIVATE PROPERTY JOBS

Male athletes can do well as a tennis pro, golf pro, or sailing pro at an exclusive club. You meet women constantly.

Women atheletes can benefit here, too. I knew an RM who met a tennis pro at his club and wanted to marry her.

Women can work the hospitality tents for country club golf tournaments, as well as part-time jobs in clubhouses.

TUTORING OR NANNY JOBS

For both men and women, music tutoring of RMs' children, governess or nanny-type work are marginal to submarginal. They sometimes work out, but usually not. You are often considered to be too much in service to them.

Yes, I know sometimes these jobs work out—but consider other ways that don't tie you down to a relationship with someone other than the RM.

PROMOTION JOBS

Jobs with some independence and status are best for both men and women.

Public-relations jobs are good, as are outside sales jobs with exclusive hotels.

SALESCLERK JOBS

Sales jobs in stores typically do not reap well, although I understand that Neiman-Marcus has a pretty good track record.

EDUCATIONAL JOBS

Schoolteaching rates low for meeting the Rich, but in a very small or rural community, it can be a plus socially with the Rich. In very small or rural communities education equates with status as much as money does.

If teaching is your hot button, though, at least get into a private school with blue-blood students. Sometimes the pay is lower; sometimes it is higher. But your motives for teaching there are temporarily more important than pay.

Check the children's registration cards to see which children are from divorced parents. Request a private conference with the parent of the opposite sex and state a reason, related to helping the child, why it was important to see that particular parent. Be positive about the child.

Another way to meet RMs, if you are teaching school, is to take evening part-time jobs as a hostess in an exclusive restaurant—especially if you are in or near a city.

HEALTH-RELATED JOBS

Many women have become nurses in order to meet and marry a doctor. Smart thinking in a lot of ways; however, many nurses do not marry doctors.

As a nurse, you want to choose your health-care facilities carefully so that you are in the hospitals the Rich frequent. These can include alcohol and drug rehabilitation clinics.

Private care can get you inside—but that's a health-sitter situation that may or may not get you anywhere. However, when someone is dependent upon your care, they tend to begin caring back.

STARVING ELITE

Just because you are a lawyer or a doctor doesn't mean you are making money. The title, however, can give you entrée to debutantes as well as grande dames in widowhood.

In fact, numerous male CPAs, stockbrokers, realtors, and lawyers and physicians are ambitious individuals who want to marry money for the silk-stocking trade it brings them.

9

Meet the Rich for Free

> Don't give to or do anything for an RM that the RM can hire someone to do.
>
> —GINIE POLO SAYLES

The preceding chapter tells you how to meet your RM and get paid for it. Now, how about how to meet the Rich for *free?*

TEMPLES OF THE RICH

The denominations and religions favored by the Rich are the Episcopal denomination and the Jewish religion. You can attend both!

HOSPITALS OF THE RICH

For men, volunteer for charities the Rich support, for hospitals the Rich use, for churches the Rich frequent. It's just possible you could be mobbed by lonely wealthy ladies who yearn for an understanding heart.

Realize these charities do not exist for your social life, so do excellent volunteer work. No one can be attracted to someone they don't respect. Anyone is expected to do good work for pay; but the person who does excellent work without pay and for charity is considered a person of quality. And be reliable. Better still, be indispensable.

ART SOCIETIES

For women, volunteer for charities and arts—and, yes, network with women you meet there for men to date. It gives you entrée to social events where you will meet RMs. They will likely be with dates, but read Chapter 12 to handle that situation.

POLITICAL PARTIES

If you only have time for one volunteer effort, volunteer for political parties. Try to get on committees, especially steering committees. You can meet the powers behind the thrones there.

10

Meet the Rich Socially

> Marrying the Rich is like marrying Santa Claus and getting into his toy bag all year round.
>
> —GINIE POLO SAYLES

This is my least favorite way to suggest your meeting an RM because you have to *pay* your very own precious money to get into the social event, and you may go there and still not meet anybody! Too, the real socializing among them will take place privately.

Buy the most exclusive opening night tickets that include a social afterward to the major performing arts events. *Opening nights only*!! This allows anyone who buys an expensive ticket to meet certain cast members and feel en rapport with the financial lords of the land.

The Rich know they are being used as bait to tantalize the Would-Be Rich. In fact, these charity organizations sell many such tickets and refer to it as Snob-Appeal selling.

Snob Appeal means that people go places simply because the Rich go there. They want to be able to say they did such-and-such that the Rich did. And, there's nothing wrong with that.

11

Meeting the Rich by Design

Take the money and don't run. Stick around for more.

—GINIE POLO SAYLES

When you want to meet a person by design, that means *you must learn to be deliberate.*

Strategy is your mental game. You must not fear being outrageous in your ploys because they frequently are the very ones that work the best.

OBITUARIES

Study obituaries, wait six months, and follow up with a strategy to meet the person. Locate the widower's office, if you're a woman, and apply for a job (even if you have different job qualifications).

If you're with certain financial institutions, you can cold-call the day you read the obituary. If you are truly good with investments you can genuinely help the grieving person. There are professionals who do this and make a fortune by handling the person's account.

A woman friend of mine said that she appreciated a stockbroker calling her on the day her husband's death was announced. She said that she was worried more about how to handle the money he'd left her than anything else. She said, "My stockbroker saved my life, financially. I was relieved when he called."

The grieving survivor is vulnerable to help because they are confused and worried about what to do now. Someone appears out of the blue with a sense of authority and who seems to know what he/she is doing and survivors allow themselves to be guided through it.

A woman on the West Coast read in the obituaries that a wealthy man's wife had died. She waited a few months and then telephoned. Posing as a free-lance journalist, she asked for an interview for a publication in his industry.

She asked if she might interview him one evening because of her schedule.

The gentleman consented and welcomed her into his home and into his library for an hour's interview. She couldn't even take shorthand, but she poised her notebook on her knee and made short scribble marks from time to time. She asked him questions, guiding him to reveal important, useful information about himself, his deceased wife, and their life together. She also asked about his children and other family.

As she stood to leave, he said, "You know, my family doesn't like for me to talk about all this. I've had it bottled up inside and you've been good for me tonight. Would you mind if we have dinner sometime soon?"

She gave him her telephone number and said she also might call him if she needed to clarify anything. This was smart. If, for some reason, he decided to not call, *she* would have a reason to.

Well, he did call. They did go to dinner. They married some months later.

How to Read the Obits

The first thing you must understand is that you are not going to find a wealthy prospect every time you pick up the obituaries.

The second thing is, you may find a prospect who is too old. The surviving spouse may be virtually senile (yes, I know you don't care, but the point is that the surviving spouse may not even be able to remember your name, much less marry you).

Third, you must be knowledgeable about which organizations require considerable money to join as well as prestigious recommendations in order to join; or require the giving of large sums of money; or connections to join.

Too, know the churches, synagogues, et cetera, that attract the Fat Cat memberships. The section on Society Pages in this chapter tells you how to get a good idea as to which clubs have moneyed club memberships.

Usually, if there is a big write-up, the deceased was important in some way to the community, to history, to society, to the country, to the world. In most cases, that translates into big money being left behind.

Not always, of course; because the person may have been noted for a particular heroic act or award but settled into a quiet, happy life that didn't require a lot of money for enjoyment.

But, by and large, if someone is being covered for free in a story by the newspaper apart from the tiny-print obituary that someone has to pay for, then the person usually had financial prestige.

Note the words in italics in the following sample.

Sample Newspaper Column Obits

RITES SET FOR JACK JACKSON III

Services will be Monday for Jack Jackson III, a prominent Major City businessman.

Mr. Jackson, 58, died of a heart attack Saturday at Major City Hospital. His funeral will be at 1 p.m. at St. John's Episcopal Church.

In 1959, Mr. Jackson, a Major City native, started the Jackson Manufacturing Co., which specialized in government aircraft con-

tracts. He also *founded* the Jackson Children's Retreat on a section of the sprawling 15,000-acre Jackson Ranch in Montana.

The *privately funded* retreat serves as an environmental therapy service for troubled children, ages 7 to 12, and offers a variety of domestic and *exotic animals*. The retreat has been a haven for hundreds of children over the 12 years since its inception.

Mr. Jackson, who was born in

Major City, received a bachelor of arts degree from *Yale* in 1948.

He was a member of the *Redwild Club*, the Major City Country Club, and *St. John's Episcopal Church*.

He is survived by his wife, Mame Jackson of Major City, a sister, Mrs. Edwina Jackson Phelps, and his father, Jack Jackson, Jr.

Men who are checking the obits can easily see that Mrs. Jackson is likely no older than 55 to 65—and over 60 is not too likely. And, who knows, she may have been considerably younger than Mr. Jackson. At any rate, chances are, she is probably a widow who is fairly well off.

His name, alone—Jack Jackson III—the "third" has a lofty sound of inheritance in it. Often, the tradition of inheriting a name into the numbers is found among those who are also inheriting money from the first one, Jack Jackson I!!—and properly tie the name with the money in its chain of command from originator to inheritor.

A manufacturing company that specializes in government aircraft contracts should be lucrative. Not only that, but anyone who "founds" something is usually a leader and so has some impressive connections.

The fact that it is founded on his goodly sized ranch indicates money. Exotic animals are expensive!

His education at Yale cost a lot and his connections from Yale probably yielded expensive connections, as well.

His membership in the Redwild Club is something that you have to know for yourself as to whether it is an exclusive, prestigious club in your community. If you don't know that, find out (see "Society Pages" in this chapter).

Too, if the particular Episcopal church listed is *The* prestigious Episcopal church of your community, then you know the old boy was simpatico with other Rich who pray there.

Although money is attracted to the Episcopal denomination, not just every Episcopal church has moneyed genuflectors.

This is true of country clubs, too. Be sure you know

which clubs, country clubs, and churches or synagogues are the places where power money plays and prays.

You might have some concern that Jack's father is still alive and ties up some of the money, still, as does a sister; but, from the look of things, Jack was a Wealth-Building heir (Chapter 15) and made money himself.

No children were mentioned as survivors, which means less interference from others in the marriage-romance you have in mind for the widow. Plus it probably means more money for the two of you.

Tiny Print Obits

Don't overlook the tiny-print obits! There are many wealthy people in very large cities who are only noted in death through such obituaries. Note italicized words.

Sample Tiny-Print Column Obits

LINDENMOST—Grace Ellen, on Dec. 31, 1990. Wife of Simon. A memorial tribute to be announced at a later date. Contributions in her memory may be made to the opera company of your choice.

LINDENMOST—Grace Ellen. Sinclair Masson, the Board of Directors, singers, and administration of the Major City Opera Company deeply mourn the passing of Grace Ellen Lindenmost, a beloved friend and longtime *supporter* of the company. Her *ongoing generosity* and devotion to the arts has nurtured not only the Major City Opera Company but also *innumerable other arts organizations.* Her effect will long be felt throughout the art world. The Major City Opera extends its deepest condolence to her loved ones at this hour.

LINDENMOST—Grace Ellen. The Board of Directors, faculty, staff, and students of the School of American Opera grieve the loss of Grace Ellen Lindenmost, devotee and *patron*, and are indebted to her *generous encouragement* and *support.*

A quick scan of this dear lady's obituary notices tells you that Simon is probably one rich widower. In fact, it may have been dear Simon's money that so endeared Grace Ellen as a contributor to the opera company.

The fact that three paid obituary columns are dedicated to this woman is, in itself, eye-catching.

But the fact that two of the obituary tributes are paid for by: (1) A major opera house, whose existence is paid for by contributors; and (2) a school of opera whose furtherance is also sustained by donors, lets you know that this was a patron of hefty sums.

The language itself, and the words in italics paint a picture of a woman who was Social Rich—a desirable level of rich, to be sure.

But to top it off, the second obit lets you know she paid her way into many top social events with deep-pocket donations to "innumerable other arts organizations." Simon Lindenmost is a most desirable candidate for your interest.

One thing missing here is any mention of her age—although the obit refers to her "longtime" generosity, so she is probably middle-aged or past.

Now, you know that in order to meet Simon, you can likely get into volunteer memberships for the Major City Opera Company or telephone the opera company for a story on the dear lady and ask how you can reach her husband or children for a comment.

You may be more successful with an *indirect* approach. You could telephone the opera company and say you are conducting educational research (working on a doctorate, writing a book or a novel) on the opera.

You can ask if there are back issues of their in-house magazines that you can come to the opera and research. If so, I assure you some issues will pay tribute to Grace Ellen or to the couple.

In fact, the first opera given by the company that is performed after her demise will likely have a write-up about her in their program.

Her widowed husband may attend the opera if there will be some tribute made in her honor (not likely, but possible. You can inquire.).

And, you can research Grace Ellen and Simon Lindenmost's name in the Major City Library newspaper society pages for an idea of other events they were active in.

Use Your Noggin

Then you must use your own noggin to find a way to get into an event or to telephone or to apply for a job or to be in his neighborhood and create a reason to inquire at his house for assistance—at a time you believe him to be home (see "How to Meet a Specific Person" in this chapter).

If you know where he lives, you can quietly follow him to see where he goes at certain times and then go those places yourself, looking as gorgeous as possible and positioning yourself where he can see you. You can even take a date as a prop.

You can also say, "Excuse me, aren't you Simon Lindenmost? I met you briefly at a Major City Opera Company" (name an event you read he attended). Then ask him a question that is not a yes or no question, so he has to answer you in a sentence or a string of sentences.

You then comment on his reply and develop it into a conversation. Be sure to mention something you always admired about his interest or his profession. Hand him your personal card, smile, and say, "Excuse me, I must go· but, I've enjoyed seeing you again." Then, leave and join your date or leave the premises, et cetera.

No, there is no guarantee that he will call, but if you do this with enough obit leads, you'll likely find some takers.

In sum, when reading obits, look for the following:

1. Names you recognize as prominent;
2. If not names you recognize as prominent, then clues as to financial standing, such as:
   (a) Private schools or impressive schooling;
   (b) Ownership of business;
   (c) Titles that indicate inheritance or social standing with tradition;

> (d) Founderships or foundations;
> (e) Patron contributions or other philanthropy;
> (f) Arts organizations, charities, the right churches or synagogues; and
> (g) Clubs and memberships that require money or prestige to join.

3. Age (old is okay as long as pre-senile);
4. Survivors—how much will the pie be divided up?

DIVORCE RECORDS

Some cities do publish public records of divorces, while others do not. A famous movie star was recuperating at a spa, and she deliberately read the records, looking for marriage leads.

Sure enough, she came across the divorce of a very wealthy man I dated sometime later. She telephoned him and they began seeing each other. Although he didn't marry her, the ploy worked well enough for her to enjoy an excellent date life with him. And since he was going through a divorce, which isn't easy for anyone, he was glad she saw it and called.

When you read divorce records, look for names you know that are Rich. Otherwise, have your telephone directory beside you to look up an address, if listed. The house is probably being sold; but the neighborhood can give you a good idea of financial wherewithal.

If the person is not listed in the telephone directory, you can always go to the library and check the City Directory.

MEETING A SPECIFIC PERSON

This requires some investigating and then some positioning on your part. Also, you can practice whatever you intend to do on someone you're not interested in, in order to work the bugs out before trying it on the person you're interested in.

Gather Information

Study the RM you want to meet. Read everything you can about the RM. Read the love lives, study the ex-spouses. See if there is a type of man or woman this RM has a history of falling for.

One wealthy man dated a lot of models but his wives had all been brainy types. Surely enough, when he married again, his new wife was an intellectual.

Learn the RM's Physical Hot Button

This may take a little detective work on your part—including taking a day or two off work in order to follow the RM to see where she or he goes to lunch, works out, has tea, et cetera.

Mind you, you may not know where the RM lives, which may be necessary in order to do this. Read Chapter 14 for ways to find out.

Many times, though, you luck into hearing about a restaurant where a certain celebrity or wealthy person has lunch or dinner.

In either case, once you know where the person goes, observe the person from a distance to see what type of person the RM *responds to*. Never, never believe what an RM has said or is quoted as having said he or she likes in the opposite sex. People may say what they think is expected of them. Their responses do not! Believe *only* what the RM responds to.

Once you've determined what you believe to be the RM's hot button, then alter your image accordingly.

Bait the Hook

Dress in the clothing style that equals the class quality this RM responds to. Your clothing is your first body language to an observer; so let it say what you are.

Position Yourself to Be Seen

If it's a restaurant, sit in clear view of the RM. I mention restaurants a lot because the RM is going to be there a minimum of 30 minutes, probably, and possibly longer. You have more time to work with.

Be Approachable

Go alone to the restaurant because you are more approachable alone. However, you want the RM to see your personality.

Use the waiter as a prop.

You are not "familiar" with the waiter; nevertheless, you quietly ask the waiter questions about the menu, and respond at least once with soft laughter. I don't care if the waiter simply says, "Yes, it's served with hollandaise sauce," laugh. You want the energy of your face, body, and interaction to make you noticeable.

Pretest

If you feel too nervous about your ploy, then try it out on someone else that you are less interested in. This way, you can work the bugs out and develop greater confidence in the messages you are sending.

Just see if you can do it.

Variations on the Theme

If tracking down your RM's lunch habits is impossible, but you are able to find another turf, then take all this same strategy and apply it appropriately to that setting.

I was told of one woman who found out by accident where a celebrity lived on the beach. Knowing his weakness for young, shapely bodies, she donned a skimpy bikini and parked her own young, shapely body on the sand outside his house.

Day after day she came in bright bikinis. She stretched and angled her body in provocative ways as if she were merely sunning and considered herself to be alone.

After a few weeks of this, his butler appeared at her side one day, with an invitation from the celebrity for lunch.

GET ON PRESTIGIOUS MAILING LISTS

Get out your yellow pages telephone directory. Telephone and get your name on the mailing lists of art galleries, performing arts theaters, humanities and historical groups and as many associations and organizations and political groups as you can. You can stumble across some interesting events while you sift through the information.

CRASH A PARTY

If you crash a party, there are two rules to follow. First, be sure it is a large party, not a small gathering or dinner party. Second, crash *quietly*.

Once you have quietly crashed a few parties, other people who see you there won't know you crashed and they will think you *belong* there. Then they automatically put you on their invitation list to their parties and soon you're not crashing anymore. A friend of mine had major success with this system.

The preferred way to crash a party is to know who is giving the party, although I crashed a party successfully without knowing who was giving it and it turned out well.

If you know who is giving the party and the occasion, then dress appropriately, fill your pocket or purse with elegant personal cards, which are the size of a business card and contain only your name and your telephone number (not work number, not address).

Getting In

Wait until the event is well under way, then enter. Don't look at the person who is taking up invitations. Walk past casually.

If you are stopped, you can say you have already checked in and turn before being asked your name and go into the crowd.

Or, you can say you are looking for someone and you'll return in a minute. If you are asked to supply the name, give the name of the host. If you are asked to wait while the invitation-taker fetches him, you have two choices.

First, you can use that time to leave. Second, if the party is very large, once the invitation-taker disappears into the crowd (unless there is someone assisting him/her), you can disappear into the crowd, also, in a different direction, hoping not to encounter the person.

If you do encounter the invitation-taker, act as if you are trying to find him or her to tell them you've already given your message to the host (or to someone else to give to the host and thank the invitation-taker for his/her trouble).

Turn as if you are leaving, move rapidly ahead and away, and in the direction that indicates you are leaving the event. When you are far enough ahead, duck in a different direction.

However, if you watch carefully at the time you arrive to crash, you can usually find a time when the person taking up invitations is either engrossed or you can find another means of entering. You can even see a few people returning from the restroom or some area near you and simply walk as if you are with them into the party—continuing on past them once inside.

Once in the Party

Before you go to the party, anticipate party talk. After all, the whole point of crashing a party is to meet people—which means talking to them.

Be very smooth and casual about introducing yourself to people as a way of meeting them. Be observant of situations during the party that you can make comments on to someone as a way of starting a brief conversation that shows your charm and allows you to introduce yourself.

Anticipate that those who do not know you will likely be curious as to how you know the host. Prepare an answer that logically fits.

If, say, you have read about Mr. Super Duper in the society pages and know that he is active in supporting the opera, don't say that you met him through the opera.

Very likely the person you are talking to is also active in the opera and knows anyone Mr. Duper knows. Questions about it could cause problems.

Instead, you may say that you and Super (use his first name) met through a mutual friend. If asked the name of the friend, and I doubt you will be, make up a name and add, "from Australia—Do you know him?" Naturally, the answer will be no.

Just smile and say, "A dear person," and then ask a question that the person cannot answer with a simple yes or no. Respond charmingly to the talk, and move on to other people.

Lingering too long not only kills a person's interest in you, but it can also lead to conversation that would give you away.

Only if a particular rapport builds between you and someone there will you offer to give your card, saying, "I've enjoyed talking to you. Before I go, I'd like to give you my personal card." When they take it, smile, and move on to other people.

It's best if you know what your host looks like so you can avoid him. Also, don't overstay because, again, that increases your chances of getting caught.

Crashable Parties

Parties that are among the easiest to crash are those that are given in large hotel ballrooms and large outdoor garden parties on the accessible grounds of a mansion. Also, if you have tickets to a special event (perhaps an arts event) that has a party following it and your ticket does not include an invitation to the party, crash.

One way to find parties to crash is by cruising such areas during party seasons, such as Christmas, Halloween (costumes make your chances even better), New Year's Eve, the Fourth of July. These are high alcohol consumption events, and people who are drinking are less likely to notice irregularities, which makes it easier for you in every way.

Also, newspapers frequently pre-announce galas and balls. Being in the right neighborhood allows you to hear about a specific party that someone is giving.

DATING SERVICES

You can join dating services and specify Rich. Some dating services have fairly well-heeled clientele. Be sure you check with the Better Business Bureau and get references from the dating services and check the references before you shell out your own money.

TAILGATE

Be a subtle private eye. Don't snoop, but follow impressive-looking couples and see where they go. Go there yourself.

Track down a license plate number if you're able and figure out a way to meet the person.

PERSONAL ADS

Place personal ads. I suggest you place 3 different ads at one time and see which one pulls.

In all ads, include your age range, weight, height, hair and eye color.

Ad 1: Specify your interest in marriage and money and tell what you have to offer as a spouse of someone Rich.

Ad 2: Don't specify your interest in marriage at all. Instead, do specify your interest in money. Then depict yourself as very glamorous and desirable. However, you are a bit elusive and looking for that right match that can hold you down. This can be *great!*

Ad 3: Don't specify either marriage or money. Instead, specify the life-style you anticipate as part of the relationship. Keep it specific and short—i.e., a mansion, complete with butler and chauffeur. Be sure to say you are not very good at doting on others yourself.

Have the paper publishing the ad use their address or a blind box address. Never have your address or telephone number published.

When You Respond to an Ad

Talk by telephone first and meet in a public place in the daytime and in a non-mood-altering situation, not in bars.

When you talk by telephone, only talk a few minutes. Many people kill the potential of the relationship by telling too much to each other on the telephone and then get together the first time and have nothing to say.

Frankly, I suggest you have a friend go separately to the place where you are meeting the person. (You may want to choose a friend of the opposite sex, since a same-sex friend might just decide to meet the person.)

You and your friend will agree in advance not to say anything to each other. Your friend is only there as a safety net, to note a complete description of the person you are meeting.

You may want to have an agreement with a friend that you do this favor for each other.

While talking to the person you are meeting, gather information you can verify, and verify it!

If a person will lie to you about his/her work, the person will probably lie to you about a lot of other things. So telephone the personnel office of the company listed on the business card, or that he or she has mentioned.

Pretend to be someone else—a loan officer or something—and verify the person's position. However, the person could have given you someone else's card, so mention a brief description.

"John Doe, a young, blond male, applied for a loan with our company. He said he is president of XYZ corporation. I am verifying if he is Mr. Doe in that position."

You can also telephone and ask for the person, using a pseudonym, and when he or she answers, you can hang up if you recognize the voice. If not, verify who they are and tell them that's what you're doing. You're certainly within your rights.

Respond to ads, also, observing these guidelines:

1. All ads will ask you to send a picture of yourself. *Never* do that. The person is a stranger.
2. All ads will ask you to write a letter telling them about yourself. *Never* do that, either. The person is a stranger.

Instead, do the following:

1. Write one brief response about yourself that you will send to every ad you respond to—no matter what the ad says it wants from you.
2. Include your age range, your weight, your height, hair and eye color.

Sample:

Hi—I liked your ad.

I'm 5'4", black hair, blue eyes, late thirties, 111 lbs.

I have neither time nor inclination to write detailed, personal letters about myself.

Let's get acquainted by telephone—maybe meet later for nachos.

Jenny

(101) 311–1133

---

3. If you have an unusual name spelling, as I do, you may want to misspell your name for protection of your identity. You can correct that later if you get to know the person.

Again, never give your address.

SOCIETY PAGES

Usually, social sections of newspapers flash prominent or Rich smiles taken at party galas and rattle off names and locations of private clubs.

How to Verify the Quality of a Club

Telephone every private club listed in the telephone directory and inquire about membership requirements. If your name is asked, you can make up one. Then, check the society pages in the newspapers—especially the conservative or Republican-biased newspapers (they may be politically conservative but they are socially flamboyant). See if there are recognizable names attending events held in those clubs.

If you are new to a community, don't worry, you will

soon learn the names that have clout. Then you will know which names to look for.

When you come across the picture of an RM in the society pages, research the person.

Find out what their interests are. Discover where they go and go there. Read Chapter 14 to aid research.

ONE OUTRAGEOUS WAY I MET AN RM BY DESIGN

People ask me if I did things I mention in this book. Indeed I did! Many times. The one that follows contains so many elements and so many different methods rolled into one, that I have selected it to share.

One year, I had business to conclude out of town on December 31, which is an unfortunate state for New Year's Eve!

However, that evening I noticed a man in a gold Mercedes as he stopped to pick up his date. He was cute and I decided I'd like to meet him. My teenage daughter, who was with me, took down his license plate number as I followed the car to see where they were going, so we could go there.

They went to a private party on the top floor of an office building. By the time we parked, they were inside and the door was locked. We turned to leave when an older couple emerged from the elevator and came toward the door. As they passed the door, we entered, got on the elevator, rode to the top floor, and crashed the party. We walked past the girl taking up the invitations, saying "Happy New Year!" and disappeared into the throng.

We had a lot of fun, met the host (oops—but it turned out okay), met the host's secretary who had been taking up invitations, and I even kissed a few people Happy New Year, but we never found the man and his date.

RESTRATEGIZE, IF NECESSARY

The next day, we returned to Dallas, but it bothered me that I hadn't met the man I wanted to meet.

A few days later, I traced the car tag, but it only gave the name of the car dealership who sold him the car and they wouldn't tell me his name.

So, a few weeks after the party, we telephoned the host's secretary, described the man, and asked who he was.

"Hmmm. Well, I don't know if he has a gold Mercedes or not," she said, "but that sounds just like James So-and-so."

I dialed his home number to see if a woman might answer. His answering machine came on, saying, "Hello, James isn't here right now, but if you'll leave your name and number, he'll gladly call you back."

An idea occurred to me—*a wrong number!*

LEAVE ENTICING MESSAGES ON AN ANSWERING MACHINE

I sat bolt upright. Yes, that's it—I'll leave an enticing message on his answering machine as a wrong number!

At home, I began scribbling out a script. I knew there are four things that are imperative for a woman to make known in order to get the interest of a man. Those four things are:

1. Men are extremely, extremely romantic. I knew I had to let him know that I am romantic.
2. Men want to think they have a desirable woman. He couldn't see me, so he wouldn't know if I were desirable or not; so, I knew that if he thought I was desirable to other men, he would figure I looked okay.
3. Even though he knew someone else desired me, I had to let him know that I was available.

4. Some men are conscious of an appropriate age, so I had to let him know I was in his age range.

My script contained all those ingredients. Plus, since his answering machine gave a name—James—I couldn't very well leave a wrong number unless the name happened to be the same, which wasn't very likely! Finally, I came up with the name "Jim," since Jim stands for James.

Waiting until 2 P.M. on a weekday, when I knew he was at his office, I telephoned his house. Surely enough, on came his answering machine, "Hello, James isn't here right now, but if you'll leave your name and number, he'll gladly call you back."

"What a funny message!" I said in a sparkly voice, "Hi, Jim. This is Ginie. I just wanted to thank you for flying up to Dallas for my surprise birthday party. I like being 39. (This was February. My birthday is mid-June.) But, I'm sorry about the conversation we had at the airport. Please don't be angry. . . . Call me . . . bye." Click.

Of course, he couldn't call me. He had no number. Then I waited two weeks and wrote out another script. At 2 P.M. on a weekday, I called again.

Once again, his answering machine came on, "Hello, James isn't here right now, but if you'll leave your name and number, he'll gladly call you back."

I said, "Hi, Jim. This is Ginie again. Gosh, I guess you really are mad about our conversation at the airport. You said that I don't want a real relationship, that I like single life. But that's not true. It's just that I'm so romantic. I think there should be more between two people than just friendship. You and I have been friends for so long, let's not spoil it now. Please don't be mad. Please call me . . . bye." Click.

And, of course, he couldn't call me. There was no number.

I waited another two weeks. I really didn't know what I was going to do next. I couldn't just keep leaving messages that led nowhere. I was wondering if maybe I could call and say I'd moved and had a new number and leave it. I didn't like it. I didn't know what I was going to do.

I picked up the telephone and dialed his number, thinking maybe I could get an idea as I listened to him.

His answering machine came on: "Hello, James isn't here right now, but if you'll leave your name and number, he'll gladly call you back." His voice paused, then added, "If this is Ginie, Jim said he's not mad about the conversation at the airport, but he's lost your telephone number! If you can leave your number, he'll gladly call you back."

I was absolutely *shocked*!

Shaking, I looked at the receiver and hung up. Oddly enough, the first thought that came into my head was "Nobody will ever believe me!"

So, I went to the nearest electronic store and asked if they had something that would allow me to bug my own telephone with a recorder. They did and sold me a device with a suction cup connection.

I went back home and I have it on tape!

In the meantime, though, James' machine was getting click, click, click from me before I finally left a message.

When I called back, I said, "Um, I think I must have a wrong number . . . but, my name is Ginie Polo and I'm a stockbroker at thus-and-such and my telephone number is such-and-such-and-such."

Well, he called me the very next day, said he would be in Dallas on Thursday and asked if I would meet him for a drink.

I agreed and, surely enough, at the appointed time, he arrived—and he was the *wrong man*!!!

He wasn't the man I'd followed in the Mercedes, although he certainly fit his description. I was more than surprised—I was astonished! All that work!

He was a wonderful man, though, and his family is one of the most prestigious names in Texas land holdings. We dated through the spring and summer of that year and I even spent Labor Day weekend at his ranch that September.

If he ever finds out that I met him by design, I think he'll love it and laugh, too—that's the kind of neat person he is. He did ask me the day we met if he were being set up by his friends. . . . Not by his friends, he wasn't.

12

Meeting the Rich Without Their Knowing You Did It

> You can meet the Rich without their even knowing you did it!
>
> —GINIE POLO SAYLES

Although material in this chapter can apply to either men or women, I am going to direct the strategy from a woman's point of view in meeting Rich men. That's because women in different parts of the country and of various ages may still be guiding their love lives by rules set down by a different ruling generation. And, because the older RMs they want to meet may also be operating out of the older rules.

Whatever social rules someone lives by doesn't matter a whit to me. I'm simply interested in seeing women and men get their bodies together for a fulfilling relationship, so I teach how to do it for the comfort of anyone of any social dictum in our culture.

A friend of mine stopped a man in passing, one day.

"Excuse me," she said, "but I pass you just about every day and I would like to get to know you, if you're interested."

He really hadn't noticed her before, but decided he was interested. They dated a short while, lived together six months, and married.

I hope you are comfortable meeting someone that way. It can work out well.

But there are times when you may feel uncomfortable

being direct with your interest. Just because you feel uncomfortable being direct doesn't mean you should forgo meeting the RM; so the following strategy can get you through those moments comfortably.

NANCY DREW/HARDY BOYS SLEUTHING

With this method, you approach an RM in such a way that the RM doesn't even realize you did it.

As an example, I'm going to walk you through a party setting (although you can use it just about anywhere) and tell you how to meet the person you want to meet.

On Your Way to a Party

Look fabulous (Chapter 4), and then:

1. Set a Secret Personal Goal:
Decide that you are going to initiate contact or a conversation with a minimum of eight RMs.

2. The Party is Practice:
It's your secret game with yourself. You are learning to be deliberate—so vital to achieving goals, such as meeting and marrying RMs—and you are *practicing* your skills.

Your attitude is that you are going to see if you can do it. Since it's a secret, there is no egg on your face if you don't—but, ah, what a smile of confidence steals across your face each time you carry it off.

At the Party

1. Recheck Physical Appearance in the restroom.

2. Be sure your posture is exceptionally "up and back." You can be the most noticeable person at the party just by your posture.

3. Generate a slight sense of excitement in your personality as you move through the party, spotting the RMs you want to meet.

4. Make it a numbers game. Decide to meet several RMs. Women defeat themselves by committing too quickly to an interest in one RM. You will be infinitely more successful with an RM if he eventually knows he must *earn* your commitment through marriage.

If You Want to Meet Someone Who Is with a Date

If the person is not married, then remind yourself that:

(a) You are not the American Red Cross.
(b) You also are not responsible for anyone else's relationship.
(c) You don't forgo meeting someone who could be perfect for you just because the person is with someone else.
(d) The person is not married!

You should never throw away potential happiness by presuming that you know what someone's relationship is. They may be at the party together, but:

(a) They may be blind dates.
(b) They may be friends.
(c) One may be crazy about the other, but it takes two to make it happen. If it's a one-way street, believe me, you are not going to keep them together by not making your move. They will break up anyway.
(d) They may be on the verge of breaking up.
(e) They may be tolerating each other until someone better (that's you) comes along.
(f) They may be madly in love. In that case, neither one

will even *see* you while you're talking to them, much less respond.

(g) The woman you are protecting will not like you more for it. If the shoe were on the other foot, she might take advantage of your date.

(h) If this were a job, would you neglect a promotion into the position that another woman, whom you don't know well, is going to lose whether you take it or not? Of course not. As the movie *The Godfather* states, "It's business." Ahem.

My point is—trash the guilt, don't let it trash you and your love life. It's a competitive world and you are in this world by yourself unless you do something about it.

Step-by-Step Meeting Him If He's with a Date

1. Secrecy Is Your Strongest Ally.

Once you've spotted an RM you want to meet, *don't tell anyone*! People blow their chances more times than they know by confiding their interest in someone.

For one thing, when you tell a friend, your friend wants to "help."

Even if your friend has enough sense not to say anything about your interest to anyone else, your friend may introduce you with giveaway enthusiasm or may give a transparently meaningful glance toward you.

Just knowing that you are interested can cause your friend to become awkward or self-conscious when the three of you are talking together.

It's not fair to any of you—especially you. And, it can be deadly to your goals. You want to test the water first with this RM's potential.

Let's say, you've spotted an RM who is with a date, a red-haired woman. No wedding rings. No in-love body language.

2. Collect Data Indirectly.

Go to your hostess, whom we'll call Sue, and ask about the woman who is with the man you are interested in. Do *not* ask about the man you are interested in.

Why should you not ask about the man? Well, let's see what could happen if you do. If you say, "Sue, who is that great-looking guy with the redhead?" Sue probably would respond in a slightly cool tone, "Oh, that's John . . . something . . . I can't remember. Jane Doe (the redhead) brought him."

Then, if you went on to say, "Do you know if he and Jane are simpatico? I really would like to meet him," Sue would probably force a polite smile to hide her bristling that you put her in this situation.

Her reply would likely be, "Well, dear, I really don't know how involved Jane is with him. I'll see what I can do for you . . ."

Not only have you been a beastly guest to have put her in a spot like this, but what if she really did (and I doubt she would) introduce you, or mention it to the man, or tip off Jane?

Then you still have to play out your little drama of interest under her nose. She would be fully aware of the outcome—your success or your failure—and neither one is good for your friendship with Sue.

Sue now won't trust you. She won't want to invite you to future parties; and she will inwardly sneer if you fail.

3. Utilize Relationship Psychology.

Success has its power in secrecy. Any success—but especially relationships. The less anybody knows about your love interests, the better your chances of making them happen the way you want them to.

Plus, there is a psychology, a perception of you as either being successful with the opposite sex or a failure with the opposite sex.

That perception of you is perpetuated word-of-mouth to
your benefit or to your detriment. And do you know who
builds that perception of you? You do.

Every time you tell an interest you have that doesn't pan
out, every time you tell how bad a relationship was, you
create a failure fragrance, a failure mystique that perpetuates
itself to your detriment.

Don't do it again. The Rich like winners. You will be
perceived as a winner if you don't play out your losses to a
full house.

Example for Success

Go to your hostess and say, "Sue, who is the lovely
redhead standing next to your floral vase?" You are asking
about the *woman* who is with the man you are interested in.
You haven't mentioned the man.

Sue glances, then smiles, saying, "Oh, that's Jane Doe.
Isn't she pretty, though?"

"Yes," you agree, then ask, "What does she do?"

"Jane is in real estate. A real dynamo, I've heard," Sue
says.

At this point, you switch the subject so she doesn't
wonder much about it.

"Oh, well, she looks familiar. By the way, Sue, I'm
having a marvelous time at your party."

You chat a few minutes and then go your way. When you
approach the man you are interested in meeting, completely
ignore him.

Instead, direct your attention to Jane Doe, the date of the
RM you are interested in meeting.

Looking her in the eyes, smile and extend your hand,
saying, "Jane, I'm Ginie Polo Sayles. Sue told me you are
in real estate. What company are you with?"

Sue will light up and think, "Client!" and you begin any
kind of tale for interaction that you want to.

Do not glance at or flirt with the man you are interested

in meeting. Stay focused on Jane. If you want her man, fine; but do not put her in the embarrassing position of having you flirt with each other right under her nose—and don't put her in the triumphant position of his possibly rejecting your flirtation right under her nose!

Instead, focus entirely on her—no side glances at him—and see if she intends to introduce you.

If She Doesn't Introduce You

If Jane does not introduce you (rude, but smart little cookie), continue talking a minute.

Then, still looking at Jane, say, "Well, Jane, I'm so glad I got to meet you, I hope we'll . . . Oh, excuse me! (as you 'seem' to suddenly see her date—the man you're interested in—for the first time) I'm Ginie Polo Sayles. What's your name?" to her date!

Again, no flirting. You just seem to be correcting a minor social error of not introducing yourself.

He may say, "John Smith."

You ask, "Are you in real estate with Jane?"

He may say no and tell what he does. If he just says no, but doesn't volunteer his profession, *ask.* "What do you do?"

As soon as he tells you enough for you to be able to track him down in a week or two, then say, "Well, I'm glad I met both of you. Jane, I hope to see you again sometime."

If She Introduces You

If she is polite enough to introduce you to her date, then, when you do look at him, be sure your expression is completely open-faced, totally non-flirting.

Simply extend your hand to him, saying, "It's nice to meet you, John. Are you in real estate with Jane?" If he says no and doesn't elaborate, ask, "Well, what do you do?"

As soon as he supplies his profession, you may ask one or two questions more to clarify where his office is or what his company's name is, seeming to be merely polite, then say, "That's nice. Well, I'm glad I got to meet you."

Turn your eyes and full attention back to Jane as if you are interested in her as a person and not her date, adding, "Jane, I'm so glad I met you. You're as charming as Sue said. Hope I see you again."

Immediately, *go*. No side looks at John.

You now know where he can be found during a weekday when Jane isn't around. You can begin setting strategy to be in that vicinity around noon or closing time—perhaps in the hallway, waiting for the elevator—"Didn't I meet you at Sue's party a week (a few days/weeks/etc.) ago?" Believe me, these methods can work!

If you would like a different ploy, you can also spend some time watching unseen to see where he goes after work, which happy hour, which restaurant for lunch, and so forth.

You come up with a strategy. You come up with a plan. Deploy the plan and feel the excitement when it works!

That's the fun of conquest. It's deliberate. It's a mental game. It's exciting.

If the Person You Want to Meet Is Not with a Date, But Is in a Group of People

Let's say you notice a black-haired man you want to meet. He's surrounded by a group of people, talking.

1. *Watch who he stands next to.*
In this case, let's say that standing next to him is a silver-haired man.

2. *Watch who he talks to.*
He talks to a rotund little man in the group quite a bit. He

talks to an older couple. He talks to the silver-haired gentleman . . .

3. *Wait until someone he's been talking to leaves the group. You talk to that person.*

The rotund little man moves out of the group. You walk over to him in a casual way, smile, and say, "Hi, I'm Ginie Polo Sayles. What's your name?"

(Note: It's easy to meet people you're not interested in meeting—however, give yourself points because you have successfully met this man—trying or no trying!)

He gives a sharp nod and says his name. It's obvious he thinks you're coming on to him. Please keep in mind that you don't give a damn what he thinks. He is only a source of information to you and you are talking to him for your purposes only.

4. *Ask about the person standing next to the man you want to meet.*

Ask a question about the silver-haired man who is standing next to the black-haired man you are interested in. Never ask directly about the man you are really interested in.

"I just saw you talking to the silver-haired gentleman in the group near the fireplace. Someone told me he is a lawyer. I thought he might know my brother, since my brother is a lawyer, but I don't want to embarrass myself. Do you know if he's a lawyer?"

Now he knows you're not interested in him, so you should feel better. He will probably say, "No, he's not a lawyer. He's in the newspaper business."

You say, "Oh. Hmmm . . . Well, I wonder if they were talking about the black-haired man standing next to him. Is *he* a lawyer?"

Again, he'll probably shake his head and say, "No, he's the country's largest manufacturer of tennis rackets."

5. *Change the subject and leave.*

Laughing, say, "Well, I don't know who they were talking about. I'm very glad I met you. I hope you enjoy the party" and move on.

6. *Talk to a few other people.*

Before approaching the group where your black-haired man is, go to the restroom and check your posture and grooming again. Rev up your energy level and radiate happiness.

Return to the party. Circulate and enjoy yourself awhile but soon enter the group of people where your black-haired man is.

7. *Position Yourself Next to a Person Standing on Either Side of the RM You Want to Meet.*

Once you enter the group, who do you think you'll stand next to? That's right! The silver-haired man that you're not interested in.

You could stand next to the person on the other side of the black-haired man, but you already have information about the silver-haired man that gives you a natural conversation tool.

You move into the circle of people, forcing yourself to stand exactly *in line* with everyone on both sides of you—not a little behind the line of people, which seems timid (Chapter 3).

8. *Do Not Look at the RM You Are Interested In.*

Sip your drink. Glance about. Wait for a natural wedge in the talk if everyone else is talking.

When the silver-haired man next to you is silent, turn slightly to him and quietly say, "Someone told me you are in the newspaper business. What part of the business are you in?" (Or, "Do you broker newspaper companies?" or "What is the name of your paper?")

This gets you quietly included in the talk. Gradually widen your talk to include people on the other side of you.

9. *Become Part of the Party Chat Until You Are Able Inconspicuously to "Drop Your Key Word."*

At some point, someone will ask you a question about you. At that point, you just happen to mention something about tennis.

You won't even have to worry about how to meet your black-haired man then. Everyone in the group will immediately direct your attention to him. You can naturally discuss his business and even ask for a card before you leave.

GIMMICKS

Gimmicks are for fun. Gimmicks seem to be most successful when you are:

1. Between trains—that is, between relationships.
2. Have a relationship or relationships going but you're not sure where the relationship is going or you feel there is something missing.
3. Have a sense of mischief so that even if you have a relationship that is secure, you just like the game of testing to see if you can make something happen, if you can pull something off and get away with it.

However, be prepared that the gimmicks may not work. That's the thrill of it all—that it may or it may not work.

One gimmick that did *not* work for me the first time I tried it—but that *did* work for me the second time I tried it, was ticktacktoe.

One of my girlfriends and I went to a popular and unbelievably crowded club one night. There were no tables and we were lucky to be able to inch our way up to the bar.

Standing next to me was a well-dressed, good-looking

man (I think they're all good-looking) who seemed to be
preoccupied.

"How can I meet this man," I wondered. He seemed
completely absorbed in his own thoughts, as if he weren't
even there.

Casting about for an idea, I realized that I didn't want to
just say something to him. I wanted to do something
different. If it worked, fine. If it didn't, fine.

Taking a pen from my purse, I drew two vertical bars
crossed by two horizontal bars on a cocktail napkin. I placed
an X on one of the spaces, put the pen on top of it and
scooted it in front of him.

He looked at it, smiled, picked up the pen, put an O on a
space, replaced the pen on the napkin, and scooted it back in
front of me.

Back and forth we went playing ticktacktoe without a
word. At last he won—and he really did win—I don't "let"
men win.

He stepped back from the bar, looking me full in the face
with a broad smile while he dug in his pocket, took out a
wad of money, placed it on the bar next to his glass, turned
and walked out!

So it didn't work. That's the risk. But how bad a risk was
it? Who cared? It was fun and kind of funny, whether he
responded or not. It was more interesting to my own
self-image than a successful coup that was ordinary.

A few weeks later, my girlfriend and I went out again.

This particular club was so cavernous and so pitch-black
that I wasn't surprised when time passed and we hadn't met
anyone.

Thinking of what to do, I recalled my ticktacktoe effort
and, once again, drew a ticktacktoe bar on a cocktail napkin.
Calling the waiter over, I handed him both the napkin and
my pen.

"See this?" I asked. He nodded. "Give it to . . .
anybody!" I said, with a shrug.

He nodded again, turned, and disappeared into the darkness.

A few minutes later, two dark figures emerged from the blackness and moved toward us. All I could think of was the title "Creatures from the Black Lagoon," and held my breath.

They were terrific. They introduced themselves, sat down, and the one with the ticktacktoe napkin finished the game with me.

My friend and I ended up dating these two men. So it worked this time. Again, if it hadn't, it was still worth a try.

HOW TO HANDLE REJECTION

1. First realize that it really has nothing to do with you. That's the truth.

You don't know what is going on in the life of the person you are flirting with or interacting with:

(a) He or she may have a major business loss in hand.
(b) The RM may be seriously involved with someone else and wouldn't respond to he ghost of Marilyn Monroe.
(c) The person may have recently experienced a bitter relationship and wishes to take it out on someone else.

Whatever it is—the "readiness" factor—that all-important element—is missing, and there is nothing you can do about it, no matter how hard you try. It's no reflection on you.

2. The minute you experience that shriveling feeling of being rejected, not good enough, ineffective, foolish in your inner self, immediately realize that it isn't you, *and* immediately convert the experience into "just practice!"

The person didn't count anyway because you were just practicing. Anyone who doesn't respond—and even those who do—are just practice until something solid develops. And, if you keep practicing, something *will* develop!

3. Immediately and deliberately interact with three or four other people within the vicinity who weren't around when you interacted with the other person. Do this for your own sake of not letting the experience defeat you.

You are learning. You are growing. One of the best examples is given by Barbara Sher in her book *Wishcraft*, in which she says that if a little baby scolded itself after a fall, it would never learn how to walk.

Instead, the baby gets up again and, fall or no fall, keeps working at it until it learns to walk. Do the same thing as you interrelate with the opposite sex. Get up and interact again!

There are so many fun ideas you can come up with that you'll laugh whether they work or not.

You can leave cleverly designed, enticing messages on an RM's answering machine. I did this with an RM and had wonderful success.

Don't do anything in your pursuit of an RM that embodies criminal dishonesty or serious character dishonesty. Certainly nothing serious enough to damage a relationship if known. Funny, clever ploys that are flattering to the person being met are best. The pursuit of an RM should be approached with humor and fun and the instinct of a gambler—willing to risk losing for the chance to win!

13

Your First Conversation with an RM

What to Say and Not Say

> You have to create a challenge as early as possible in your first conversation with an RM.
>
> —GINIE POLO SAYLES

Once you are face-to-face with your RMs, *how* do you *meet* them?

Even if your RM is a celebrity, conversation rules are basically the same as with anyone else. You *say* something. You speak in the same manner you would to anyone else (see Chapter 3).

Before you approach an RM be sure you:

1. Maintain great posture.
2. Have an energetic walk.
3. Wear an expression of happiness on your face.
4. Speak to other people you wouldn't normally say anything to so you seem casual when you speak to the RM.

It doesn't matter what you say, just as long as you say something—and, just as long as it is even mildly appropriate.

How will you know if it is appropriate? It is appropriate if it is:

1. Related to what is going on in the situation;
2. Said with a light cheerfulness; and
3. You either keep moving or pause with body language

131

that shows you are only pausing, not stopping to try to make a relationship out of it on the spot.

This is your manner with everyone, including RMs—with one . . . little . . . hitch. You create a *challenge* as early as possible in the conversation with an RM.

If you are just "nice," the RM won't remember you. If you can raise a small challenge to your RM by something you say during your initial conversation, you will stand out.

If presenting a challenge is not your forte, then you must find some interesting way to stand out that separates you from everyone else there. The Rich seek the unique—not the run-of-the-mill, ordinary person.

Remember that Aristotle Onassis said to never try to please the Rich. Why? Because everyone is trying to please them.

Servants are paid to please them. Social climbers and investment or service brokers too often become sycophants, trying to please, please, please the Rich.

Only their equals do not try to please them. In order to be an equal or at least to appear an equal—which is a must for your goals—then you must set yourself apart from the servants, investment and service brokers, and social climbers who pander, smile, and nod, and go along with the Rich.

If the RM is a celebrity, it is especially important to stay with down-to-earth human interest talk that you have in common—children, hometowns, school days, et cetera.

Above all, don't ask for an autograph. Don't even mention "Who He/She Is." That makes you just another fan, not an equal.

On the other hand, you must not be rude. Rudeness labels you as lower social class, period. You simply don't try to please.

You may mention a particular work the RM did—a movie or some such, and comment that you liked it and tell why (with intelligence). Then ask a question the RM cannot answer with a simple yes or no and that has nothing to do with the RM's celebrity status.

Emphasize what you have in common during your initial conversation to build rapport—an interest in opera, say.

It's just as important, though, to point out cute ways that you are different from your RM to stimulate interest and to show that you complement each other.

Always be the first to end a conversation and to move away to talk to others or to leave.

CREATING INITIAL CHALLENGE

Some very simple ways you can create a challenge follow through conversation:

1. Gather information about your RM from others who have been talking to your RM—without letting them be aware that you are interested in your RM (very important; see Chapter 12).

Then you can casually interject a comment into a later conversation that your RM is involved in, knowing full well that your RM will respond to it. This is your RM's hot button.

2. Creating a mild challenge is to put your RM on the defensive by listening closely to a position your RM takes on something, and disagree.

Be sure you can back up your opposite position with an unusual viewpoint that creates interest.

Do so in a manner that is not haughty. Also, disagree only on *one* topic or you'll just seem like a disagreeable person, period, and that's boorish, not challenging.

3. You can place a small wager with your RM on something being discussed that will have an outcome within a few days.

This gives you a perfect excuse to call—especially if you

lose the bet. You can call and insist on paying your dues over cocktails or coffee.

Or if your RM loses, call and insist he or she pay it over cocktails or coffee.

4. Don't talk all the time, but do talk. Ask questions from time to time. Look into your RM's eyes as he or she talks and respond in a natural way.

5. Occasionally do not respond, so that your RM values your approval.

6. Talk about human interest topics. You don't have to say anything funny or profound or even half-bright! Think of how *People* magazine focuses on people interests and sells! That's what you do.

7. Weather, food, children, and events that are going on are all good fillers. Spotlight the interesting, novel side of people issues.

8. Be basically honest, but never admit your life is empty or depict yourself as bored or lonely.

Always seem to have a life you enjoy, filled to the brim with events and projects you are excited about.

9. That's why you must *never* poor-mouth. Once a relationship has begun you gradually break into your RM's piggy bank with simple financial expectations that you speak up and express—but not for a while.

10. And have a purpose in life—or seem to have a purpose. Don't just be obviously waiting for Daddy or Mama Big Bucks to come along and save you from poverty.

That *may be* exactly what you are doing, but don't let it show. Pretend to have a project you're working on—a novel you're writing, an invention—something that can take you a long time—years, even!

11. Find subtle ways to point up your special qualities and abilities. You know yourself that you're impressed when you discover something unusual about someone who otherwise seems ordinary. Do this for yourself to *sell yourself.*

12. And, whereas you are nice about others, you should be smart enough not to praise another man or woman who could become your competitor.

It does not make you look noble. It's dumb. If anything is mentioned about someone, acknowledge the person nicely, and turn your RM's attention elsewhere.

13. Never brag about goals you have or plans you are making. You have made a fool of yourself if something prevents it. Remember secrecy is your greatest ally. Instead, do it in secret, then reveal it in a casual way that knocks the socks off your RM.

14. Negative pessimism, a critical nature—all are out! You keep your conversation and outlook positive and upbeat and sometimes, just sometimes, mysterious.

15. The most important advice you can ever take is to never, never, never tell how badly anyone has treated you—especially not ex-spouses or former lovers.

If you do so, you are describing:

(a) how little the person respected you;
(b) how little you respected yourself to put up with it; and
(c) what you will put up with in a relationship. You may be swearing you won't put up with it again. Listen, relationships aren't that easy to get out of once you're in them. And everybody is nice at first!

SELECTIVE TRUTH

Instead, give your RM something to live up to. When the inevitable question "What happened to your last relationship?" is asked, *fudge!*

Say that the person you were with was really very good to you and that he or she was a wonderful person. Tell what I call "selective truth." The good truth is just as true as the bad truth. And, frankly, if you are harping on the bad truth, then you're being just as selective about the truth, anyway, only in a negative sense.

Then give some benign reason or have amnesia or say you don't discuss previous relationships. Blame a job change, a move to another state, PMS, or anything you want to, just don't say, "My mate cheated on me, stole my money, beat the kids, and kicked the dog."

I know we've all had rotten relationships and we've all made the mistake of confessing our souls to someone who didn't turn out any better. But that's my point.

BREAK THE PATTERN

Haven't you ever seen men and women who have "patterns" in their relationships? They always marry someone who beats them, or who runs around on them, or something awful.

Well, it's because they told the new person about the last person. The new person thinks, "Well, if he cared enough about a woman who treated him that way, then he's going to have to prove to me that he cares even more for me than he did for her by putting up with worse behavior from me than she gave him!"

Many of my clients have discovered that this one principle alone has done more to change their relationship patterns than anything else.

Now, if you feel distressed that this prevents real, true

honesty and breast-baring intimacy, don't worry. I think it's fine to tell them the full story—three years after you're married and your relationship patterns are already formed. Even then, tell the truth a little at a time in very small doses!

THEY DON'T LIKE LOSERS

Very few RMs will treat you any better than the last relationship you describe.

The RM will usually end up treating you the same way because your RM knows you've taken it before, so you will probably take it again.

You sound like a loser and Rich people are funny that way—they don't like losers.

16. Always be the first to end your initial conversation with an RM. Either move away to talk to someone else or leave.

14

How Do You Know
if an RM Is For Real?

> Watch the way men interact with other men and
> you can tell which one is Rich more by the
> interaction than by anything he is wearing.
>
> —GINIE POLO SAYLES

If you carry on a long-distance relationship, or if you are
not around a person very often, you are subject to being
fooled by a professing RM.

To keep from wasting time, though, you will want to
check out an RM as best as you can. The following
guidelines are not foolproof; but they're better than nothing.
They can help you check out a person you have met or track
down someone you want to meet.

CAN THE RM DELIVER?

This, to me, is ultimately the best way to check out a
person. Can or will the RM deliver?

You have compassion for a person; but if they are leading
you on, you test their ability to perform by:

1. Making suggestions of what you want to do.
2. Upgrading the RM's suggestions.

MAKING SUGGESTIONS

Name the very most expensive restaurant in town. When
your RM takes you there, order all of the most expensive
items in every category of the menu. This can include two

items, even. If the RM winces or goes to the restroom or
complains of being on a diet or suggests you order something else, you have your answer.

UPGRADING YOUR RM'S SUGGESTIONS

Let's say an RM suggests having a picnic together. You
light up and say, "I'd love it. Why don't I have the Epicure
Elite Caterers pack an elegant gourmet picnic for two that you
can pick up on your way after me. And, to make it more
exciting, I'll telephone in for reservations on your card for a
flight to Puerto Vallarta. We can have a romantic picnic for
two on the beach. We can make it there and back in a matter
of hours!"

True, an RM may have commitments that prevent being
able to spontaneously hop on a jet for a gourmet picnic with
you in Puerto Vallarta.

However, if, *every time* an RM suggests something, you
then upgrade the setting for it, you'll find out very quickly
if real money is available or not. And, frankly, if the person
is Rich but you're not going to benefit, then why bother?

The only other recourse with someone who may have
money but not share it is if you know the RM has other Rich
and generous friends. In that case, use the hell out of the RM
to get you around the friends who have potential and make
the time count toward cultivating one of them for dating
toward marriage (or whatever your goals are).

NEIGHBORHOOD

This may or may not be a reliable method of determining
whether a person has real money. The individual may be
house-sitting, or using someone's corporate-owned house,
ranch, apartment, or condominium.

You can check the deed records at your county court-
house to verify who owns the house.

If the person rents an apartment, how expensive are the

apartments? How exclusive? This may be an apartment rented by a corporation for guests or out-of-town officers to use when visiting, so don't come to any conclusions until you've checked further.

Again, you can check the city directory, which is listed under the heading "Library" in this chapter.

2. Check the clubs they belong to. Normally, if a professing RM takes you to a club that you know is very exclusive, and if the RM is known by people in the club, or you see the RM's membership card, consider it a positive indication. However, look for other indicators to confirm it.

IN THE LIBRARY

In the reference section of your library you may be able to check the company your prospective RM professes to own or to be an officer in. Many of the following publications list the officers of the corporation, as well as providing a health report on the company.

Look in the front of the directory for instructions on specific ways to use it. Some of the directories you will want to learn to use include:

1. The City Directory—a cross reference, listing the people in a city in three categories:

(a) Address: You can look an address up and find out who lives at that address.
(b) Name: You can look up the name of a person and find out where the person lives.
(c) Telephone: You can look up a listed telephone number and find out whose it is.

Often the City Directory gives the marital status by giving the name of the spouse as resident, occupation, and sometimes lists the telephone number.

2. The Telephone Directory—Look up the company the person professes to own or work with and telephone

personnel, pretending to be someone else. You may say you are with a lending agency or with a social club and just verifying the person's position for membership or lending.

If there is a telephone number listed, call and see if a man or woman answers. Ask if it is Mr. or Mrs. So-and-So.

3. Dun & Bradstreet Million Dollar Directory™ of America's Leading Public & Private Companies—provides information on more than 160,000 top businesses.

4. Standard & Poor Register of Corporations is more detailed. It includes the name of the company, address, and telephone number, tne Chairman of the Board, lists all officers, gives the company's primary bank, accountants, law firm representing them, sales volume, and number of employees.

5. Macmillan Directory of Leading Private Companies.

The following directories may be helpful, depending on whether you are tracking an RM that you want to meet or if you want to verify a person's professed status.

Usually, each of the following directories has an index that you will want to use first to locate the year or volume in which your RM may be listed. Listing does not mean the person is Rich, however, just notable for some reason:

1. Finance in Industry
2. Current Biographies
3. Webster's American Biographies
4. Who's Who in Politics
5. Who's Who in America
6. Contemporary Newsmakers
7. The Directory of National Biography

If you want to check out someone who is "closer to home":

1. Investigative industry surveys are usually published as a book or professional reports. Most industries have an industry report that provides basic information about companies in that industry.

Investigative industry surveys are broken down by

industry, such as iron, petroleum, physicians, lawyers, et cetera.

Directory Pluses:

(a) An investigative survey in the industry in which a person purports to be an RM can merely verify the RM is in that industry, if listed. It doesn't mean the RM is successful.
(b) Investigative surveys or reports may be published for each state.

Directory Minuses:

(a) Not everybody who is active in an industry will be listed in a directory; so it's still possible your RM is for real and for some reason isn't named.
(b) Some listings are voluntary.
(c) A few legitimate RMs will forgo being listed because they know that many sales people use the directories as a telephone or mail solicitation tool.
(d) Not every library carries an investigative industry survey. Telephone before you go to see if there is a publication on the industry you are interested in that lists the people or companies in that industry.

2. Encyclopedia of Associations

If you can't find information about someone in the profession the person claims, look up the professional association in the Encyclopedia of Associations. Telephone the association for that field. Using a different name, if you like, call and ask how you can verify if someone is who they say they are in that profession.

3. Newspaper Microfiche

Major newspapers keep their back copies on microfiche. You can check their index, see if a person in your area has had anything written about him/her and read up.

There is an index for the *New York Times*. Large public libraries may have microfiche for some newspapers, but many do not.

4. Magazine Indexes

Magazine articles of virtually any time period can be tracked down through an index system known as The Reader's Guide.

5. Ask your librarian if there is a local or regional Who's Who. There are usually statewide or regional directories, such as Personalities of The South, et cetera.

6. Some libraries offer a research service for a small fee. Find out what types of information and areas they research before you say what you want. Their methods of research may provide an indirect way—i.e., through the type of business or hobby the RM gave you—for you to verify that your RM is for real.

A PRIVATE EYE

This costs money; however, if it's important for you to know about the person, then comparatively shop private investigative services.

Try to find someone who is either a new investigator or who has just gone into business for herself/himself. These people need the business and may give very cheap rates.

Know exactly what information you want and how you will be charged.

If you hire an investigator, keep your information profile simple. All you want to know is if the person is for real and possibly if the person is married or involved.

If you get too detailed on the person, I think that smacks more as rotten of your character than the possibility of it in the person you are checking.

You can also find out a little bit by following the person for a while; but, really, I think that's a waste of time, demeaning, and you feel like a snoop.

Your time is better spent looking for other RMs, while seeing if this person can deliver.

15

Types of Rich

You can and should judge people by their hearts and not their money; but the Rich are going to marry somebody, why not you?

—GINIE POLO SAYLES

HOW RICH IS RICH?

D Magazine of Dallas, Texas, had an article in their 1990 special issue on Power, that partly defined Rich as the ability to borrow. That's a good definition.

The premise of this book has been that Basic Rich begins with one million dollars net worth apart from home and personal belongings.

Net Worth is the value of an RM's resources after you subtract what the RM owes on what he's borrowed.

RMs who have substantially more net than debt create an RM style I refer to as Net Rich.

RMs who are so highly leveraged (borrowed) that they live glamorous life-styles while juggling assets create an RM style I refer to as Debt Rich.

They are one step ahead of creditors and one step only—not substantially. They are as risky as a junk bond and might be better termed Junk Rich.

Now, don't start panicking that you might end up dating someone who is Debt Rich instead of Net Rich. Believe me, you won't be able to tell the difference and the Debt Rich can be worth more money to you in some cases than the Net Rich.

The Debt Rich, who are life-style-conscious, will treat

145

you well. They want to impress you with their wealth as much as they want to impress anyone. They can be fun, lavish, and they take you places and introduce you to people who can help you. Too, you will meet other RMs while with them.

There is also the possibility that a Debt Rich personality will get far enough ahead of the debts to become Net Rich.

Since you won't be able to tell which Rich is which, just hustle so that you get everything you can while the getting is good.

Whatever type of Rich your RM is won't matter as long as your own debts and life-style are paid for by the RM. Just be sure you have put aside what you can get out of them in gifts and money to keep you independent of them.

PROFILES OF RMS

People cannot be absolutely categorized. However, there are some general profiles that can be useful for identifying RMs.

Men who are seeking an RM have four basic choices:

1. Rich Divorcées
2. Rich Widows
3. Rich Heiresses
4. Rich Women Executives or Entrepreneurs

Rich Divorcée

The Rich Divorcée may have helped her husband succeed. However, on their way up the ladder, they grew apart. One or both had affairs, which eventually led to divorce.

This RM is the easiest to find. She frequents popular bars, goes to Happy Hour, joins clubs, goes to parties, takes trips, all in hope of finding another husband and to fight off loneliness.

She is outgoing, dresses expensively with a style that is halfway between preppy and sophisticated.

Be sure she lives on income from assets, not alimony, or she won't marry you until the alimony runs out—and that defeats your purpose.

Rich Widow

The Rich Widow tends to dress in preppy or traditional styles. She is usually more conservative in her social behavior out of a true reverence for her late husband. She considers it a responsibility to uphold his name and memory. This RM mostly networks among her Rich friends and relatives for men to date.

Begin asking friends if they know wealthy widows or if they know someone who knows someone who knows a wealthy widow to whom they can introduce you. You may have to live in her husband's shadow, but it may be worth it.

WHAT THEY HAVE IN COMMON

As different as they are, the Rich Divorcée and the Rich Widow have certain things in common.

Both spent their married years developing the social life for their families. Among the ways they did this was through charity work, art societies, and other similar avenues.

Initially, they may have built their identities in these organizations partly to please their husbands and to further their husbands' careers in a social contest.

However, as their husbands' careers reached a point of success that no longer required the business leverage of social contacts, their husbands lost interest and increasingly declined to attend events they now considered boring, leaving their wives to attend them alone.

Their husbands' loss of interest came as a blow of

rejection to the women. More than ever, they continued to cling to this one area of unrecognized success that had been a key to their husbands' career, which now shines with success.

The identities of these women are built in these organizations, which are mostly filled with other women like themselves. That is all the sadder, since the women are now single.

Your Key with the Divorcee or Widow RM

The Rich Divorcée or the Rich Widow longs to have a man to share her interests, to appreciate what she has contributed, to recognize her achievements. She wants to "show off" for him in a harmless way, and, most of all, to have him *spend time* with her in her interests. She won't mind buying the tickets to these events and gradually undertaking more expense for a man who seems to be sincerely interested in her and in her art and charity social world.

You will encourage her to pursue special events from her past interests and you will be willing and ready to escort her on a moment's notice. From these special events you get a firsthand look at how she is treated by others and you meet her wealthy friends.

Rich Heiress

Rich Heiresses fall into two categories.

Wealth-Conscious. This is the woman whose inherited wealth and position is her only identity. Furthermore, she only associates with peers. Unless you have a blueblood history or are already in her social and financial circle, you'd better . . . forget her.

Crusader/Rebel. These RMs date, befriend, even marry people not of their social station. They have a heart and make good wives, period. Try not to take crass advantage of them. They're good women!

Your Key with the Crusader Heiress RM

Portray the sincere, quality man she believes you to be. Play up the fact that you are one of the undeserving downtrodden, who only needs someone to defend him, believe in him, support him.

Use the words "ethics," "honor," "integrity," and "honesty" a lot.

Rich Women Executive/Entrepreneurs

A Rich Woman Executive/Entrepreneur is very, very, very, very busy. This woman is *not* just posing as a career woman, she is serious about making money and achieving goals. She won't mind helping you do the same. She considers having the best in life to include having a good husband. If you can fit into her plans, you stand a good chance.

There are three types of Rich Women Executive Entrepreneurs.

The first type will want *you* to have a career of your own and to be successful on your own, too.

The second type will find a House-Husband okay with her. She won't be picky about your background, either. She simply wants love and a stable home foundation for her demanding life.

The third type will be looking for a part-time or full-time business partner, who will work alongside her to create a joint business success as well as marriage success. She will assess you on your business sense and whether or not you complement each other and pick up the slack where the other has weaknesses.

Your Key with Women Executive/Entrepreneur RMs

In any of the three cases, you must be extremely *interested in* and *nurturing of* her goals so that you become a necessary part of her overall success and happiness.

All three types are looking for a husband who is an emotional support system. They find the demands of the business world challenging enough and do not want a husband who is a problem or who tries to compete. You will find her equally as supportive of you.

RICH MEN

Can you tell if a man has money by the shoes he wears or the watch he has? A lot of women use this standard (as well as the car he drives).

Realize that a Faking RM can buy these items at resale shops, even so-called estate sales that are really upscale neighborhood garage sales. In some cases they can borrow or lease items.

Hone your awareness of Rich Men so well that you can tell the difference *by the way they interact with other men.*

Women who are seeking an RM can learn to distinguish the differences of behavior exhibited by two basic categories of Rich Men—

1. The Self-Made RM
2. The Rich Heir

The Self-Made RM

The self-made RM may or may not have rough edges. Usually he has worked hard on self-improvement as his business dealings brought him into contact with polished businessmen.

He memorized and practiced etiquette from books and

relied on an ex-wife to teach him why to appreciate ballet, which he doesn't attend anymore but buys unused corporate tickets for each year. He has extensive and expensive memberships in everything that requires success to join.

He has clear-cut ideas and opinions. His presence dominates a room even if he is standing still because his high-risk nature and aggressiveness are difficult to hide.

He is forthright, dresses conservatively, and is more animated than Rich Heirs. He is dynamic, intense—this is an exciting man!

This RM is *very* marriageable. His life is built around succeeding financially and he does not want any distraction from it. He wants a wife to provide a day-to-day continuity that allows him to concentrate fully on his accomplishments.

He probably will do less cheating than any other type of man. He doesn't have the time, the patience, or the interest in it. He especially doesn't want the distractions of it.

Much later, that may or may not happen if the marriage goes awry; but marriage will always be important to this man. Should divorce or death interrupt that basic security of marriage, he will quickly replace that position with another wife—sooner than most other men.

Your Key with the Self-Made RM

The self-made RM wants to be proud of his wife. He wants her to take care of herself, to be as beautiful as possible, to be ambitious and to spend money to look good so he looks good. He expects her to be the social extension of himself and to provide a respectable, interesting home life.

The Rich Heir

There are two categories of Rich Heirs:
1. **The Wastrel.**
2. **The Wealth Builder**

The Wastrel. The Wastrel may have dabbled at a few financial interests, but, basically, he's bored. He doesn't have to work and he doesn't. He exists to be entertained. He relishes the role of patron, which gives him some sense of importance. He may enjoy the spotlight of the press. He is something of a snob and very temperamental.

By and large, this gentleman's love of leisure and pleasure lead him to nonachievement. He wanders from one activity to another to avoid being bored. He is usually soft-looking. He does not exercise and frequently overindulges in fine food and wines. He is usually politically liberal, highly opinionated; but, sadly, without purpose.

His clothing choices are usually a bit arty—maybe even with a flashy, colorful scarf.

His entire identity is built on his self-importance due to his money.

Your Key with the Wastrel RM

If he wants a wife at all, he wants her to be a combination yes-person, maid, and mama, picking up after him and indulging him.

You may be able to save him from himself. You may not want to. But if you do, you'll certainly earn every penny of it and deserve a place in heaven next to Mother Theresa.

The Wealth Builder. The Wealth Building heir inherited money and used the money to increase or actually build a fortune of his own.

This RM is conscious of his responsibilities to family name, to his community, and to society at large. He is not as animated as the self-made RM. He limits most of his expressiveness to smiles, raised eyebrows, and nods. His body usually remains passive, contained, controlled. He is well-educated and well-connected.

His marriageability can go either way. He may be open to women of all types because he has been exposed to a lot of people and ideas and has an open mind; or he may only want a wife like his mother or sister.

Your Key with the Wealth Building RM

You really have to determine if this is an RM who will marry out of his class. If so, he falls into one of three categories.

Whichever category he falls into will have its distinctive key titled as a subkey to marriage of that category:

1. *Outcast Within His Own Class*.

The Outcast RM, Jr., may carry the most prestigious last name in the community, state, or nation. His manners, clothing, education may be impeccably in line with the social set that his family name and money has enjoyed.

And yet, for some unknown reason, this RM Jr. is just not accepted in the social group his money is equal to and the rest of his family enjoys. He finds himself near the bottom of their social pecking order.

To the unknowing world and to the rest of the community, RM Jr. is Somebody; but in his own social caliber, he is simply tolerated, but not included.

Naturally, it hurts, deeply, and he seeks solace elsewhere. He encounters a woman of a lower social class, but who, perhaps, is better-looking than most women in his family's social group.

What's more, this lower social class woman looks up to him, appreciates him, thinks he is "Somebody," whether he really is or not. His name is enough. He doesn't have to prove anything else to her.

RM Jr. knows he will never really fit in or live up to his parents' name and expectations; so he flagrantly violates their marriage codes. In a hurt attempt to thumb his nose at them, pretending not to care, he punishes them with a marriage to a woman they consider beneath them. He insults them by bestowing their prestigious last name on a woman who is an embarrassment to them.

Your Key with Outcast RM, Jr.

1. *Unacceptable.* He deliberately chooses someone who is an affront to his family. Often his marriage choice may be porno stars, strippers, nude models, scantily clad men's club cocktail hostesses, drifter poets, rock singers, drug users.

Usually, if a woman who married an RM complains that she hasn't been accepted by her husband's family, it's because her husband never was in the first place.

If he had been respected and accepted by his peers, she would have been.

2. *Guilt-Ridden Idealist*

Guilty RM, Jr., feels, for some reason, that he doesn't deserve all the wealth and luxury of his world. He never had to earn it, never experienced hardship. He looks at people around him who struggle or suffer and feels guilty. He sees poor men who have made it on their own and admires them. Again, guilt. He buys his way out of difficulties. More guilt.

His one salvation, in his own mind, to justify his money is to make it up to the world and to apologize for his wealth, by marrying out of his class. He chooses a mate compassionately, based on the potential she could have with the backing and support of his millions.

Your Key with Guilty RM, Jr.

Elevatable. She will probably be someone working toward a higher educational degree, or a hard-working single mother who is trying to make something of her life and of her child's life. She may be trying to get a new business off the ground, or developing a career in the arts.

He chooses someone his family will approve of as far as values are concerned. This person will not be an affront to his family and will likely fit in, given enough time and polishing.

3. *Bored Novelty-Seeker*

Novelty RM, Jr., is bored with the women of his social circle. He is part of the exciting business world his family handed him or that he developed out of their money. His business provides mental excitement. He expects his social life to provide an equal emotional excitement.

Novelty RM, Jr., can't help but notice that the most exciting thing going on in the lives of women of his social group is the upcoming book club or opera ball, which is boring to him. He has experienced such activities with his family all his life. He wants a woman who is a breath of fresh air in his stuffy life. He wants glamour, intelligence, ambition.

Your Key with Novelty RM, Jr.

Glamour. He will probably find a woman who is in a glamour field, such as a model or an actress. She may be struggling for financial survival, which builds admiration into the excitement she offers, because she is different from what he's used to. Because the need for novelty is part of his makeup, and because his threshold for boredom is low, Novelty RM Jr. will probably cheat more than any other RM. Variety is the spice of life to this gentleman and he can afford as much variety as he pleases.

WHICH RM IS BEST?

All these RMs may socialize with each other at certain events that draw them together; but they tend to have their own, more tightly knit groups of people who are more like themselves.

So, which type of RM is best? You will enlarge your life by opening yourself up to experience all of them to some degree. One of the Richest attitudes you can have is a tolerant, nonjudgmental appreciation for people, period.

You do not have to think the way someone else thinks. You do not have to behave the way someone else behaves. Inner Richness includes an unsuspicious willingness to *let* people be different from you.

16

The Sexual Dynamics
of Money

Flirting is the last safe sex we have, so use it to the full.

—GINIE POLO SAYLES

The subject of sex will eventually come up in any dating relationship, so be prepared for it.

You don't have to go to bed with anyone you don't want to, so don't allow anyone to pressure you into a premature liaison.

If your relationship with an RM evolves to a natural point of closeness that precedes lovemaking, remember the following key issues for protecting yourself and for protecting your relationship.

IS YOUR RM SAFE?

Because of the reality of AIDS and the HIV virus, sex can no longer be treated as a game. Sex is a life or death issue.

And AIDS is no respecter of bank accounts. Self-made multimillionaire and superstar Magic Johnson joined the victims of the HIV virus, through heterosexual activity.

The HIV virus that causes the AIDS disease may not be detectable through testing for as much as one to six months after it is contracted. Too, the virus can lay dormant for twelve years or possibly more—the exact incubation period is not yet known—in an individual, thereby giving the appearance of good health.

For these reasons, no matter how much money a potential RM has, don't go to bed with her or him until you have established that your RM is a person who is aware of AIDS and who cares about sexual safety.

See if your RM brings up the subject; if not, you bring it up. Listen very carefully to determine if this is a sexually responsible RM.

An RM who is sexually responsible will want to know if you are also sexually responsible. A sexually responsible RM will not go to bed with you casually, and will discuss the importance of safety measures. However, there is no such thing as totally safe sex, just safer sex.

If the RM reacts by playing down the AIDS epidemic, cross the RM off your list. I'm serious. If, however, the RM gives safety suggestions, still stall, until you have time to judge the RM's reliability of character. DO be informed. Read and understand the facts about AIDS and the HIV virus. Protect yourself, your life, your death. *No amount of money is worth the risk!*

STAY LOW-KEY

If you do make love with an RM, don't try to impress your RM with exotic techniques the first time. It comes across that you are trying too hard and the only people who ever try too hard are people who are in a *losing* position. Keep a healthy, natural, and low-key attitude about it.

NOT A SWAP OF SEX FOR MONEY

You can set a clear standard that a relationship with you is not a swap of sex for money by asking your RM to buy something for you. Later, give the RM a hug but say no to sex if the RM makes advances.

If your RM gives the slightest indication that the RM is entitled to make love with you since you accepted the gift, you become indignant.

"Of course not!" you say with consternation. "You bought this for me because you like me!"

NOTE: Never, ever offer to give the item back. Sell it, if you like; but never return it.

PART III

Your Relationships
with the Rich

17

The Love Dynamics of Money

> People spend their money emotionally, so money-spending is a very accurate barometer of an RM's emotions for you.
>
> —GINIE POLO SAYLES

MONEY IS A LANGUAGE

For years I've been teaching that money is a language. Just recently, the scientific community has begun saying the same thing.

And money is a language all its own—just as sex and love are—in this dynamic of sex, love, and money.

MONEY-SPENDING AS EMOTIONAL BAROMETER

Money Is a Symbol of the Emotional Ego, period. People spend their money emotionally. Advertisers know that. They advertise, not on the basis of logic, but to appeal to emotions.

Watch where your RM spends his or her money and you will know what is important to your RM. Since people spend their money emotionally, money-spending is a very accurate barometer of an RM's emotions—feelings—for you.

Even with everyday people this is true. If the average man tells his wife he loves her but he buys himself a new hunting rifle when she hasn't had a new dress in two years, I think we can see where his real interest is, where his real emotions are. So, you can tell what a person really cares about by where they spend their money.

The more money you invest in something, the more you have at stake in it, so the greater your sense of involvement with it, the more closely you guard it.

If you only have a few shares of Exxon stock and the stock market moves up or down 10 points, you may not watch it very closely.

If, however, you have several thousand shares of Exxon stock and the market moves a point or two either way, you're going to know about it, because you have put so much money into it, you'll watch its every move.

You are more attentive to whatever costs you the most to have, including a person who demands the best of treatment from you over someone who will accept any circumstances you impose upon her/him.

MONEY-SPENDING PREDICTS
RELATIONSHIP CHARACTER

You can pretty well tell how a man treats people—including how he will treat you in a marriage relationship—by the way he handles his money.

One man had a pattern of wealthy, bankrupt, wealthy, bankrupt. He always used his wealth as a base of credit and then extended himself well beyond his ability to pay.

Let's translate his relationships into the language of money and see that it followed the same exact format.

(a) He was a person who made promises carelessly to women in his life. *In the language of money, this equates to buying items on a credit card.*

(b) The trusting women often built their lives on his promises to them. *In the language of money, this equates to giving him a line of credit.*

(c) But, he was never really there for them, when they needed him to come through on what he had promised in the relationships. *In the language of money, this equates to not paying when the bills (promises) are due.*

(d) Bitter endings of the relationships ensued in which the lives of the women were damaged through scandal or severe financial difficulties. He, on the other hand, went about virtually unharmed. *In the language of money, this equates to filing for bankruptcy—the creditor, who believed in him, ends up holding the bag.*

This was a man who was emotionally bankrupt. It was a matter of character, mirrored in the way he spent his money.

I am not saying that a man or woman who files for bankruptcy is a weak financial or relationship risk. There can be factors in the economy, rather than factors in the RM's character, that are the cause.

Typically, though, if an RM is cautious with money, the RM is cautious with relationships. If the RM is careless with money, the RM is careless with relationships. If the RM is there for the creditors, the RM will likely be there for you.

May I suggest strong scrutiny of how they spend their money as to how you will be treated in a marriage relationship?

MONEY IS A SOCIAL-FINANCIAL IDENTITY

People use their money to say "who they are," according to what they can afford to do and to have.

Career women often have more relationship problems with men who are not Rich.

The reason is that such men have not attained their own financial identities.

For example, a man she is involved with, who has no money, may have ambition, and may truly love her and sincerely want to nurture her career goals. However, because he is also trying to succeed, he has all the same career problems she has, so he isn't able to help her very much with hers.

He suffers inner conflict when she begins succeeding—especially if his own career is not going as well.

He is proud of her. At the same time, he may compare his

success with hers in his own mind and feel in second place (she doesn't feel that way . . . he does).

This can lead to resentments, compensations in affairs, sabotage of her efforts or of their relationship, guilt that he wishes she would fail, enjoyment of any small defeat she experiences.

It isn't diabolical or intentional. It's, frankly, a very natural, human response. Unfortunately, it breeds competition— and competition strives for the defeat of the other person. *Sad.*

A Rich Man, on the other hand, has already attained his financial-social identity and is not striving to establish who he is. Because he's secure in his social-financial identity, he enjoys the success of the woman he is in a relationship with. He often enjoys helping her succeed.

MONEY HAS RELATIONSHIP POWER

People use their money to get the relationships they want. On the *Sally Jessy Raphael* show, my husband surprised me by confessing that he had consciously used money to entice me into a relationship with him. RMs are no dummies. They know what they want and don't mind the cost if they want it enough.

RMs who say they avoid gold diggers just haven't found one they want badly enough. The idea that "you get what you pay for" operates in them, subconsciously. They may date gold diggers and just not attribute the name to them.

MONEY IS A MUSCLE

There is a **Money Macho** among men. Having money to satisfy survival needs has replaced having muscle to slay the animal beast of cave-man days. Money slays the financial beast.

A wealthy man may be slight of build, but have tremendous financial muscle. For a woman to align herself with a wealthy man can be a form of protection.

Women have sought money for independence and equality. Increasingly, though, money is losing gender, while maintaining its muscularity for both sexes.

18

How to Get the RM's Money into You

The more money an RM spends on you, the more value you have in the RM's eyes.

—GINIE POLO SAYLES

The more money an RM puts into you, the more value you have in the RM's eyes and so the better your RM treats you.

To increase your chances of getting large sums of money and exquisite gifts from your RM, be sure you implant the image in your RM's mind that you are to have the best.

HAVE YOUR RM ALWAYS ASSOCIATE YOU WITH THE BEST

Let your RM know that you expect the finest. If your RM suggests an activity, you upgrade the setting for the activity so it will be expensive.

Let's say that your RM telephones that he or she is coming into town and would you make room reservations. Then you do so in the most exclusive hotel with a lovely suite.

In this way, when your RM thinks of you, the RM will associate you with elegance and expensive quality. If you put your RM in a family motel near the airport in a nice room, your RM will associate you with that exact quality.

In your RM's mind, you become the quality you surround your relationship with. Make it a lush, first-class quality.

DON'T BE TOO EASY TO PLEASE

If you want your RM's money, you must motivate your RM's emotions of (1.) desire to please you, (2.) responsibility to you in a relationship, (3.) to avoid guilt if the RM doesn't do so, and (4.) the potential—not necessarily the actuality—the potential—of happier sex. Make them earn your approval.

YOU HAVE TO ASK

How do you get an RM's money into you? You *ask* for it.

If You Are Turned Down

If you are turned down, turn cool toward the RM. Eventually, ask for something again. If you are turned down this time, give logical reasons why the RM should do so.

Shame the RM for the comparative difference between your two life-styles and how it must look to others who see you and how they must consider the RM a low-classed cheapskate (this should rankle).

Tell the RM your time is valuable and it is impossible for you to keep up standards for dating the RM on your small income as compared to your RM's. Dating the RM is actually a hardship on you and the RM should be ashamed to take advantage of someone who has been such an asset to the RM.

If the RM is passive to your reasoning manner, select another time and say it again with all the angry, raw emotion your little heart can muster. Throw a tantrum. Remember, you are fighting for your rights in the relationship and it can net you a lot of benefits and income—or it will end the whole relationship.

Do you want the relationship if it isn't paying off? If so, *why*??

Give the RM three opportunities to pay for something

you ask for. Forget this RM if nothing is forthcoming that you request. And don't let the RM put you on hold with delays and postponements.

HOW TO ASK

1. *Incentive Buying.* Start by suggesting your RM buy sexy lingerie. This is as true for a man courting a female RM as for a female who is dating a male RM. A man can ask his Rich female to surprise him with bedroom clothes in silk for both of them. Lingerie is "bait" because there is something in it for the RM.

2. *Small Delights.* Shift your suggestions from lingerie into other small requests and gradually, over time, increase the costs and the frequency of asking.

3. *Positive Suggestion.* Try lighting up and saying, "I want you to buy that for me," or "I thought you might like to buy thus-and-such for me."

4. *Confident Tone.* Don't ask in a begging or whining or childish way.

5. *No Question About It.* State your request rather than asking it.

6. *Anticipation.* Speak confidently with a sense of excitement that the answer is going to be yes.

7. *Witnesses Motivate.* Make your request in front of a salesperson or in front of an RM's peer (This is so-o-o bad, but can be quite effective).

8. *Not a Loan.* Never "borrow" or act as if it is a loan. The benefit of an RM is to circumvent banks! You have no principal or interest to repay and no credit hassles!

9. *Withhold Sex.* Remember, even though this is not a swap of sex for money—and you don't have to go to bed with someone after receiving a gift—you most certainly never go to bed with a person if you are turned down! (Your feelings are hurt.)

10. *Reward the RM.* Hugs, sweet kisses, praise, and sometimes even excitement are in order when you receive something.

For serious living-expense help, I used to have my RMs take me on a moonlight picnic. Then I would tell them my cost of living as opposed to my income, saying that I knew they wanted to know so they could help me. We would talk out arrangements and I would put it into action the next day.

Unfortunately for men, the double standard still applies.

Have an excuse why you cannot pay your way. Your money is tied up, you helped a friend, or you're helping your mother, children, et cetera.

Be romantic beyond belief! Memorize travel brochures, study travel videos of exotic trips. Spin wonderful fantasies as you talk to her, using the travel brochure descriptions of places you would like to be with her, of moments you could share together . . . *if only* . . . you had the money!

Once she begins drooling over these fantasies of you kissing her in the moonlight in an exotic setting, she'll find a way to pay for the trip and save your manly pride at the same time.

When she does suggest paying for it, be sure you react in the following manner. Frown and think about it for a second (Only a second—don't wait too long) without a word. Then take her in your arms and tell her how wonderful she is!

Never protest that "Oh, you just couldn't" or she may see your point, and, oh, you just may not!

Get her involved in your financial projects as soon as possible. Share your ideas for expansion. Get her excited with possibilities, be enthusiastic about her suggestions, and get her name and her money into it!

Once a sexual relationship has begun—and sometimes before that—you can let her know that you would love to take her to her favorite restaurant, but you're just not able to at the moment.

It is important that during this time you have also been accompanying her to places that are her major interest—say, the ballet; and that you have been doing your homework and can share her interest—even if you're faking it. This will encourage her to be more generous with you.

If Your RM Offers

If an RM offers something to you financially, *take it.* Only turn it down if there are clearly strings attached.

For men who seek an RM, when she offers to pay your way somewhere for the first time, this is what your behavior should be: Pause. Look away in deep thought. Frown. Then take her in your arms and tell her how wonderful she is!

If you say, "Oh, I just couldn't," she might see your point and you might not get the money.

Take the money and don't run. Stick around for more.

Never feel bad that you have taken money from an RM whether you feel anything for the person or not. Realize:

1. They will spend it anyway.
2. You were a terrific asset to them during the time you spent with them.
3. Someone else will get it if you don't.

Let me repeat—with feeling—*someone else will get it if you don't*!

19

Sugar Daddies and
Saccharine Daddies
and Mommas

> Money expresses an RM's feelings more than sex
> does.
>
> —GINIE POLO SAYLES

When does taking money from your RM make him/her
your Sugar Daddy or Sugar Momma? Is it once sex and
money both start flowing?

Well, remember, you don't have to have sex with an RM
in order to get money. You really don't. There were some
RMs I never went to bed with and still received money and
gifts.

However, if you really like an RM you probably will go
to bed with him because you want to.

But, bed or no bed, money expresses his feelings more
than sex does; and, sex or no sex, I use the term Sugar
Daddy and Sugar Momma to make a few points about the
relationship once money becomes involved.

And it's at this point that you must not neglect certain
warning signs that differentiate between the Sugar Daddies
with Marriage Potential and the Saccharine Daddies with
None!

SUGAR DADDIES/SUGAR MOMMAS

Sugar Daddies/Sugar Mommas are RMs who are marriageable. They use money as an expression of their

173

emotional ego, an expression of themselves, to deepen the relationship. Money becomes their nurturing tool.

Saccharine Daddies/Saccharine Mommas are not marriageable, no matter how they may try to make you think they are (which is why you need to be able to know the difference for yourself).

For Saccharine Daddies and Saccharine Mommas, money is a substitute for themselves in a relationship, rather than an expression of themselves.

How can you know the difference between an RM's commitment of money as "self" in marriage; and an RM's commitment of money that *substitutes* for "self" in marriage?

SACCHARINE DADDIES/SACCHARINE MOMMAS

Saccharine Daddies and Mommas will use money to substitute for themselves (their "self") in the following ways:

1. The amount of money outlaid to you will plateau early in the relationship.
2. Gifts and money will sometimes be sent with a note that the RM can't make it to an event that was scheduled with you.
3. Your RM will resist giving more money than the early plateau level.
4. Your RM may give money to your enterprises but will not jointly tie his/her name to it.
5. Your RM may put money into your enterprises as an investment only (making you think he/she is being generous, but actually not) so that you actually end up giving money back through profits, which makes it a payoff for the RM.
6. Your RM will resist the idea of living together, although he/she may agree to travel with you.

7. Your RM will resist letting you use his/her credit cards or his/her name.
8. Your RM may include you in certain activities but not all of his/her social life. Usually there will be a certain group of friends you associate with; however, there are other friends the RM socializes with, without you.

Sugar Daddies and Mommas will commit money as a development toward committing to marriage in the following ways:

1. There will be a gradual and increasing level of money put into you.
2. The time you and your RM spend together will increase.
3. Your RM will put her/his dollar and name into joint ventures with you if you are at all business-minded and will try to direct you to good advice (which the RM offers to pay for).
4. Your RM will provide you with credit cards and let you use the RM's name.
5. Your RM will include you in all aspects of the RM's social life.
6. Your RM will not object to living together. Talk of marriage will not be taken lightly, if it is approached after a maturing of the relationship.

OWNERS, NOT LOANERS

Maybe it's the fault of the movie, *Pretty Woman,* but some RMs are now letting their dates "wear" beautiful jewelry for a specific occasion and then strip it off as soon as they are back in the car.

Do not ever allow an RM to do this to you. If jewelry is offered for you to wear to an occasion, tell your RM that you only wear what you can keep with no strings attached.

One man had jewelry in his safe that each of his successive women wore. Can you imagine his friends sniping behind his date's back, "The emeralds looked better on Katy than on her."

It's really more of a disgrace to the RM than to the woman. It's a little humiliating to the woman, and low of him.

Even in the *Pretty Woman* movie, I was disappointed that a man of the character he was supposed to represent would cruelly tantalize an impoverished woman with jewels and then take them away.

SET GOALS TO AN RM'S DADDY/MOMMA STYLE

Saccharine Daddies and Mommas are users. Fine. You can out-use a user any day. Get as much in tangible assets (gifts and cash) as you possibly can. Also, meet as many of the RM's friends who have money as you can.

Saccharine Daddies and Mommas have their uses. Keep it that way and you won't get hurt. Just don't start thinking that you can change them. You can't.

Don't start thinking there is something lacking in you that makes the RM this way. There isn't. Use the Saccharine RM, while looking for a real sweetie!

Yes, I know you want the relationship to culminate in marriage. That is your goal. But you may have to work your way through a few losses before you hit your home run.

Don't worry, taking money from an RM has absolutely nothing to do with the RM's decision not to marry you—and don't let one make you think it does. The RM is looking for an excuse and is lying, if that's what the RM says.

The person who gives the most, cares the most. Money-giving tends to increase as the RM gets more serious about marrying you.

20

How to Love
the Rich and Win

> Your RM will not like you or appreciate you one
> bit more for making life easier for him or her.
>
> —Ginie Polo Sayles

Once you have begun dating your RM, you will control
the relationship if you control yourself. Naturally, that's
easier said than done.

Keep your manner cheerful, warm, and not trying to
please. Then *set standards*. Otherwise, you become a boring
doormat and you will lose the RM.

The *beginning* of a relationship is the time to set
standards. The standards will become self-perpetuating as
time goes by. That's why it's important to get money into
you early.

You will be setting standards, anyway, by the way you
allow an RM to treat you. It's just that they are either high,
medium, or low standards.

For example: no matter how crazy you are about your
RM, you *never* allow the RM to come over late at night if
the RM has been somewhere without you. The reason for
this is simple.

Your RM may *say* there is a business meeting or a
business dinner or that he or she has to be out of town, and
then may telephone you around midnight or slightly later,
saying how much he or she has missed you and wants to see
you.

Don't believe it. In all probability, your RM had a date
with someone and it ended early or didn't culminate in sex
or the RM was bored or rebuffed.

177

Whatever the reason—and don't get sucked into the triviality of caring about the reason—the fact is that the RM is actually testing you to see what you will allow him or her to get away with, how poorly he or she can treat you.

This is the time to set standards that can put you in first place by demanding first-place treatment.

It's really best if you don't answer the telephone on a night your RM has postponed being with you. If you are asked about it the next day, say you had a business meeting or business dinner. Never confess otherwise.

If you do answer the telephone, say that you will not ever see him or her at that hour and that you are insulted at the suggestion.

Say good-bye, hang up the telephone and chew your pillow to shreds if you have to in order not to call back or give in.

This is really only a test of nerves and whoever has the better nerves is in control.

Whatever treatment you want, set it into your expectations, early. It's virtually impossible to change it once the patterns are set.

Men, even if you're not the macho type, come up with at least one area of relating to this woman in which you can be "tough." Just one is all it takes to establish you as having backbone.

Maybe you flatly refuse to get things for her. Maybe you openly refuse to stop seeing other women until you're married. *Something*. Just something. (See Chapter 20.)

Your manner should be that of a considerate escort, but not of a lackey.

Save up enough money to take her anywhere she requests the first few times you take her out so that she can see you know how to handle yourself and to control the dining-out experience together.

If you're a fairly young man, rent the video of "40 Carats" starring Liv Ullmann, study it, and go for the older, Rich woman.

Persistence is your key word here *and* a total disinterest in women your age or younger. No glimpses at shapely young twenty-year-olds. No second looks at passing miniskirts.

All men would do well to read Danielle Steele novels to get an idea of the secret yearnings of a wealthy woman's heart.

Be protective of her. Whatever she tells you, be on *her* side. Make her feel safe and trusting.

DON'T GIVE IN TO GIVING

Whoever gives the most, loves the most. Gauge your RM's affections for you by seeing if the RM gives to your demands.

But, if you want your RM's love to grow, you will induce your RM to keep giving more than you. This is important for marriage.

I'm not talking about overwhelming your RM initially before love has a chance to grow. No. You start out on a high expectation, which you express by suggesting the best places for your RM to take you.

Then you increase your expectations gradually (but consistently), asking in little ways, so that your RM is having to meet your needs, your requests.

As your own feelings deepen, you will have to fight your desire to "do for" your RM, your desire to please your RM, your desire to give, give, give to whatever you think will make your RM happy.

This is not being ugly. This is necessary because everyone you are in competition with is giving, giving, giving, and being used, used, used, and passed over.

You can show a giving nature by expressing your love for animals, children, senior citizens. Your RM will adore you for that type of heart. But to give to your RM is an open door for poor treatment.

For instance, a Rich man may even invite you as his date to his parties so you will clean up afterward. Yes, that's a cheapskate thing to do, but it's more common than you think.

A Rich woman may have you bartending parties all night long, when she could have hired a bartender.

Money doesn't automatically create standards in an RM—*you* do!

Setting standards means not tolerating treatment that even slightly smacks of second-class.

You are not the cook, the cleaning lady, the bartender, the laundry person, the call girl or the gigolo. Make that clear if there is the slightest implication that your RM "expects" you to do anything.

Your RM will not like you or appreciate you one bit more for making life easier for him or her. The RM will treat you the way you teach the RM to treat you.

You will be respected for refusing to do work the RM can hire others to do.

I repeat, don't give what the RM can hire others to do. Give only what the RM can't buy—a stimulating, warm, loving, and challenging relationship, packaged to look good, demanding respect.

If you're a woman, make it clear you choose not to pay your way, if the subject comes up by him—and that you don't have to pay your way. Other options are open to you.

SETTING PRECEDENTS

Be careful what precedent you set. If you start off being willing to go to the RM's house for a date, you can't expect that pattern to change.

If, on the other hand, you accept a date and then set a time you expect the RM to come to your house or apartment, you

are setting a precedent that demands something of the RM
in order to be with you. You are more special.

AVAILABILITY

Don't let an RM know you've broken a date to be with
him or her. There will be times when you will break a date
with someone else in order to be with your RM. A certain
amount of availability is very important to sinking into a
real relationship with an RM so that he or she begins to need
you.

However, the first time you and an RM set a date, it
should sound something like this:

RM: Do you want to have dinner tomorrow night?
You: I'd love it. Can we make it the day after tomorrow or
 Saturday?
If the RM says: I can only make it tomorrow night. Maybe
 some other time.
You say: Well . . . let's set it for 8:30 instead of the usual
 7, then.

You do these things to prevent an RM putting you in the
category of being able to call at the last minute or if no one
else is available.

Also, once in a while, be busy and unable to accept or
keep a date. Not very often, though.

GIVE ORDERS

Give your RM small orders. "Get me a glass of water."
"Bring me the TV Guide." If your RM gives you orders,
balk. Do it with humor, but balk. Throw a pillow or give a
teasing look and say, "Darling, get your adorable two little
legs up and get it yourself." (Or however you want to say
it.)

If you're a woman, you can prepare dinner *once in a blue,*

blue moon, if you really, really, really love and adore gourmet cooking as a hobby; but beware the RM who gets used to having dinner at your place.

Anytime you cook for him, take him shopping with you and have him buy the groceries.

Your RM should have you out and about and in the public eye with him in glitzy five-star restaurants. These are the perks of dating an RM.

Too, you want to become recognized, if not "known" among the sets who go there. This is one way of continually cultivating other RMs by being seen by them and gradually meeting them through your RM.

21

Getting the Rich Hooked on You

> You have to learn to balance stability with being a little bit of a problem to an RM.
>
> —Ginie Polo Sayles

What do RMs want in a mate? *Most of all,* they want a mate who will add excitement or interest to their lives without embarrassment—although some will risk embarrassment over boredom.

Raw emotion is preferred to noble predictability for most RMs, as long as the stability of the marriage is not threatened. Most RMs would rather a spouse smash the chandeliers than remain passive and predictable.

The maxim, "Do *anything,* but don't bore me," is the secret of keeping any mate—but especially a Rich one!

THE IMPORTANCE OF BEING A PROBLEM

Just listen to people complain about their ex-spouses. Whatever they complain about is what kept them with the spouse so long. They stayed in there trying to figure out the solution. They may not have been particularly happy about it, but it held their interest. They weren't bored.

If the problem got out of hand, of course, the stability of the marriage was impossible to maintain and the marriage ended.

You have to learn to balance being a bit of a problem to your RM with maintaining stability in the relationship.

You can do it. And you must do it. You must be

something of a problem to your RM in order to keep him or her.

If you do not oblige your RM by being something of a problem to the RM, your RM will become a big problem to you. You can count on it.

Being the problem keeps you in control of the relationship. It keeps the RM happily on his/her toes, not bored, and keeps the relationship stimulating, interesting, satisfying, developing.

DRAMA IS IMPORTANT TO A RELATIONSHIP

What if you tuned into the television series, *Dallas,* and saw J.R. and the rest of the cast just sitting around the living room of Southfork, feet up on the coffee table, eating peanuts and drinking beer?

And what if the whole time you watched it that night, nothing else happened but that?

Would you tune in again next week to watch it? Of course not. It was boring. There was nothing going on.

You tune in to *Dallas,* or any other TV show, because of the problem. Novels and TV depend on creating "problems" to keep you hooked into tuning in or turning the page. That's what you do to keep your RM tuned in to you, too.

THE IMPORTANCE OF STABILITY

Remember, I said "balance." If the relationship degenerates into a lot of fights and constant trouble, your position is reduced to gigolo or mistress level.

The energy of the relationship then becomes conflict. It may seem to fuel sexual drives; but those relationships are in trouble.

No matter how passionate the making-up may be, and no matter how much they declare their love for each other, one person is really only using the other one for entertainment.

It is a painful, doomed relationship. The respect needed for true love is lost.

"Do anything, but don't bore me," is the RM's silent desire. Be sure you heed it—with *balance*!

HOW TO FIND AN RM'S HOT BUTTON

What are your RM's unresolved ego needs? Unresolved ego needs are the hot buttons.

You begin by finding out what troubled the RM most about an ex-spouse or lover the RM cared deeply about. It must be a relationship that had an unsatisfactory ending, that the RM is uncomfortable about, or still gets a little emotional talking about.

If the RM has been married more than once, is there a pattern of a particular problem in the marriages?

Find out if the relationship or relationships were either ended by the other person, or ended because the RM gave up, or was in a victim/losing position and got out.

The problems described in such relationships are unresolved feelings and ego needs. Use these. *Do some* of the same things yourself, only not as severely. Just a tiny bit. Or do something similar. The RM will hate it and like it at the same time. It's unfinished business. It is also familiar business.

THE IMPORTANCE OF FAMILIARITY

People respond to familiarity—even unhappy familiarity—like a bloodhound who suddenly finds the trail that carries the most familiar scent!

Let's say I wave a wand and—poof!—you are suddenly in a foreign country. You look around you and you don't know where you are. No one speaks your language. You can't read the signs on the buildings. You're lost. *This is often how people feel—sometimes for years—after a relationship ends.*

What do you do? You look for something . . . *familiar!*

Let's say that you look around you and all of a sudden you see the double golden arches—McDonald's! (I use McDonald's because it's something everyone is familiar with.)

Now, for the sake of allegory, let's say that you had never liked McDonald's (hard to believe), but let's just say you never had liked it and never would go there.

Ah, but *now*, your face lights up and you walk toward it as fast as you can . . . because it's *familiar.* You may not like it, but at least you understand it. You know what to expect. You know what is expected of you.

Once you are in the comfort of being in familiar territory, then you can begin exploring the unfamiliar grounds near and around McDonald's.

You walk a few blocks, look around, and go back to McDonald's. You do this in several directions, several times, always going back to McDonalds, which is your *point of reference.*

You are familiarizing yourself with the new territory, learning your way around. *This is the weaning-away process of starting with what is familiar and then weaning away by getting used to new familiarity.*

After a while, you will have learned your way around the new territory and will no longer have any need to go back to McDonald's. But, the fact remains that it was your *starting point.*

An RM's hot button is the unresolved ego need. It is the unfinished pain. It is the RM's emotional point of reference for relating. It is the RM's starting point for learning a new relationship. Whether either of you likes it or not, it's what the RM responds to.

WEAN AWAY—NOT CLONE

If the RM carried a torch for the ex-spouse, the behavior worked for the ex-spouse, so work it for you.

Give this tiny taste of familiar pain only to keep the RM

hooked until you can wean the RM away to your own style of love. Don't feel bad about it.

Use it *only* long enough to wean your RM into your style of love. You don't want to make the pitiful, pitiful mistake of trying to clone the other person. To do so won't work.

The relationship would only end up the same way— broken. Also, you'll feel such a terribly weakened personal identity. You want to be you and to be loved a new way—not just as a clone of the previous person.

Besides, it's not that the RM still cares about the other person; it's that the problem was never solved satisfactorily.

Therefore, you simply use some of the same methods as a tool of familiarity while you constantly introduce methods of love that are true to *your* personality, and new to your RM.

In this way you gradually get your RM familiar with your style, thereby replacing the RM's familiar old love patterns with your new, increasingly familiar, and more satisfying love patterns.

Familiarity is the key word here. You must build a new familiarity into the RM, slowly replacing what your RM has been used to—first, by actually doing some of what the RM has been used to—and second, incorporating your own, better-working values.

Using the familiar problem as a starting point for weaning is much the same way that you teach a three-year-old child something by starting with what the child understands. You start where the RM is—the hot button of unresolved ego needs.

SEARCHING FOR NEW INTERACTION FORMULA

Do not believe what an RM says that she or he wants or doesn't want in a mate. Believe only what the RM *responds* to.

You'll hear RMs complain about the mistreatment they've

received or unhappiness they felt or loss of love they've experienced with a mate.

You'll even hear the RMs believably swear they will never, never, never have anything else to do with a former mate who hurt them, or tolerate anyone who behaves the way the mate did.

Don't believe it. You'll very often find that those same RMs have remarried the former spouses two years later or married someone else who is doing all the same things.

An RM's hot button is the RM's hot button, like it or not. Use it. It's the only thing the RM will respond to until the RM is weaned away.

RELATIONSHIP I.D.

An RM may have divorced the person, but the RM hasn't divorced his or her own personality formula—thought processes and behavior patterns—that went into the relationship. That is the biggest pain of divorce.

The RM now thrashes about, inwardly, trying to create a new relationship formula of behavior—only the old ones are still operative.

One RM complained of his wife being a burden. She was dependent. Once he left her, though, he found himself worrying about her and how she was making it without him. The relationship formula consisted of her *problem* of being a burden as *also the satisfaction* of his feeling needed.

HOW TO BE A MINOR PROBLEM

Once you wean your RM away to your style of love, then endear yourself with a tiny problem that is unique to your relationship together. The problem is usually built in to what attracts the person to you.

One RM loved his wife's compassion for animals and children. Later on, however, she put pets, then children, ahead of him. This problem kept him trying to figure out what he could do to change it, to gain her approval over the other two.

One RM loved her husband's attractiveness. She felt proud to be seen with him; but that automatically made him attractive to other women, which created the threat of competition.

Another RM admired his wife's social savvy and liked the constant flurry of impressive activities and interesting, successful people she brought into his life. At the same time, she was so busy with leadership commitments in social events that she was seldom able to spend time with him in London on business.

One RM admired the high principles of the man she married. Later on, however, his principles became the source of contention.

The source of the problem is usually the same source as the admiration. The problem is built into the admiration. What the RM admires is also the problem. That keeps the challenge alive in a positive way.

Figure out what attracted the person to you, what the person admires in you. You can enhance it to become a minor problem. Minor means "able to be tolerated." Minor means something that annoys only occasionally. It creates a ripple. It does not destroy the overall balance and harmony of the relationship.

You will simply be better off if you put aside efforts to be perfect and good and simply be whatever you are, just polished.

HAVING A WEAKNESS

A weakness is different from a problem because it creates more of a major-league worry in the other person. A weakness poses a slight threat to the relationship.

Because of this, be *sure* you use your weakness much, much, much, much more sparingly than you do *being* a minor problem.

A weakness should only show itself once a year or twice at the most; otherwise, it can absolutely destroy a relationship.

However, a relationship that doesn't have the enervating rush of a weakness raising its ugly head (just when the RM thought it was safe) is vulnerable to the erosion of boredom.

To choose your weakness, you can usually pluck a handy one right out of your own bag of small neuroses. Maybe you have a weakness for the opposite sex. Maybe you drink too much occasionally. Maybe you flirt. Maybe you overspend. Maybe you lie. Maybe you're jealous.

Maybe you're a hothead. Maybe you're unreliable. Maybe you like redheads. Maybe you do things that are totally unpredictable and eyebrow-raising, like deciding to telephone from Australia because that's where you suddenly decided to go in a moment of questionable whimsy.

THE POWER OF HAVING A WEAKNESS

A weakness creates an excitement that borders on misery. Yet, it challenges the lover to resolve it for the beloved.

I have seen men leave their loyal, devoted wives of twenty years for a woman, perhaps older and less attractive, who sleeps with every man in town because the challenge to their egos of the woman's weakness is more exciting in its misery than the boredom of predictable devotion.

I'm not saying this is *right*. I'm saying this is *fact*. I don't deal with what *should* work. I deal with what *works*.

Likewise, I have seen men stay married to women who sleep with every man in town for the same reason. They just get a loyal, devoted mistress on the side. However, they don't marry the mistress. They use her to keep their marriage together.

No, I don't recommend your sleeping around, since Aids is such a risk. Frankly, that's the only reason I don't recommend it! But, I use it as an example of how important it is to generate excitement in an RM—even if it is unhappy excitement at times. But only at times! Not constantly.

THE PAYOFF

A weakness makes you human and your RM noble. Your weakness makes you interesting. It adds complexity, color, depth, and texture to your personality in a relationship.

Most of all, it gives your RM a mission—to "fix" you—which makes the RM's life more colorful, interesting.

Your weakness demands more of your RM in every way. It demands more understanding, more time, more emotion, more love, more giving. Those are qualities everyone is trying to get from a partner in a relationship. And those are also qualities that if you *asked* for, you wouldn't get, and your RM would feel imposed upon and nagged.

But your weakness stimulates those very qualities in your RM without your ever asking for it.

TIMING A WEAKNESS IS IMPORTANT

Timing is all-important when you employ your weaknesses in a relationship. There are dangers of Underuse and dangers of Overuse of your weakness. Be careful.

Underuse of Weakness: If you wait until boredom sets in, you may discover you've waited too late.

Once boredom really has taken hold to the point that the other person is indulging his/her own weaknesses to fight it off, all your desperate displays of weaknesses in the world won't endear you to your beloved. In fact, it will then grate on his/her nerves and reinforce the need to flee.

At that time, your RM will then be too interested in his/her own weaknesses to bother with yours.

Overuse of Weakness: I must warn you not to overuse a weakness. You may enjoy the attention your weakness brings you from your RM; then when the problem seems solved and attention wanes, you may fear you're losing your RM and think you have to resort to it again.

If you fall into the trap of thinking this way, then the relationship can never stabilize. A relationship that relies on turbulence as its prime energy is one-dimensional and won't grow. There has to be enough peace between two people for other traits to mesh between them into a harbor of safety for both of them.

HOW TO APPLY YOUR WEAKNESS

Once you've chosen a weakness that flatters your RM into thinking he/she can resolve your weakness for you (creating co-dependence—that is, they become emotionally dependent upon your weakness to build their egos or needs around). They are going to "rescue" you from yourself/weakness. You can respond in the following ways:

1. You respond fairly well in the beginning as you follow their corrective advice.

2. You then have one or two "backsliding" occasions, creating the drama of high emotion in a conflict, confrontation, or fight.

3. You demur and try, try again.

4. You then respond well and the relationship merges into happy interacting—you, appreciative, your RM, proud.

5. About six months down the road—or later, depending on the development of your relationship (which I can't tell you and neither can anyone else because each relationship has its own pace), you have a mild relapse into your old weakness—*mild*—but just enough to restimulate interaction about it between your RM and you.

6. Your RM is having to correct you again, having to "fix" you, fix your life, fix your life together. As long as your RM is hooked into this mode, he/she will *never* notice anyone else, even if it is a *Playboy/Playgirl* centerfold, stark naked, in front of them! You are the most involving aspect of their lives right now. The RM has been thrown for a loop and doesn't know if this can be fixed or not.

7. You are smart enough to let it be fixed—for another 12 months. And, after that, I think your best bet is to make it a 12-to-18-month relapse. Maybe even switch to a new weakness.

KNOW WHO IS IN CONTROL

You and the RM cannot both be the problem. If you are worried about whether or not the RM likes you, that means the RM is the problem. The RM is in control.

One thing is certain. Both of you cannot have the weakness. One person has to be the stabilizer, the nurturer, the forgiver, the wronged, the lover, the giver—so that the one with the weakness can bring out those strengths in the other person.

If you both display weaknesses to each other, and neither one is the safety net for the other, then you enter into game-playing, which will eventually wear out the relationship.

Showing your weakness early on puts you in control. Someone is going to control the relationship. You're in a stronger position, of course, if it's you.

STAY EXPENSIVE

Distinguish yourself from the many, many others (and, believe me, they are legion, whether or not you know about them) who are after your RM by demanding the finest of treatment, the finest of places, the finest of everything you experience together. The RM will then consider you special.

Never let your RM think she or he is better than you. If there is the slightest intonation, straighten your shoulders, deepen your voice, center your eye contact, and verbally dismantle the RM. It's better that the RM think you're too good for the RM than the other way around.

DATING CHEMISTRY

Date as many people as you can. Dating chemistry works like this: Being alone breeds being alone. Being with dates breeds being with dates.

Dating RMs breeds dating RMs. Once you date one, it'll be easier to date others. It's no mystery. Whatever behavior you perform once, you are able to repeat. The more you repeat the behavior, the more comfortable you become with it until it becomes a pattern, a natural part of you.

This is true for social behavior, including dating. If you are able to date one person, you'll be able to date another. Even though you may not want to date unless it is someone you are interested in, you may find it is to your advantage to push yourself to date anyway.

The more you date, the more comfortable you become dating. The less you date, the less comfortable you are when you do have a date. So, you begin avoidance behavior, until you spend more time alone, just wishing to meet someone you would like to date. But, if you did meet someone, it would be less likely to work out because you would be unused to dating and behave in a self-conscious, defeating way.

Practice dating people you aren't interested in. In this way, you stay comfortable and natural for the time that will come when you eventually date someone who does interest you.

Whatever we learn to become comfortable with creates an attraction of others to us in that arena. The naturalness and ease of the activity generates a kind of "chemistry" or magnetism for it.

The more you date, the more opportunities you will have for dating. This is true of dating RMs. Once you date one, it is easier to date others.

In the meantime, keep your dating skills honed by dating as many people as you can. It attracts more dates. And it adds to the challenge.

DESTRUCTIVE CHALLENGE

Some people make the mistake of trying to create the challenge by being cold and haughty. This is silly since most people identify such behavior as lower social class and phony.

No truly refined person ever acts rude to anyone or snubs someone. But it's more important not to use that method to create the challenge, because even if it works, initially, it can never bring any happiness to either of you.

You would never be able to let go and be warm and loving together, although you might want to with all your soul.

The precedent would have been set, the rules established, the roles assigned, and to change that, changes the reason the person was attracted to you in the first place, and changes the relationship.

Haven't you seen that situation all too often, yourself? In all too many relationships, the challenge is based on trying to make the other person love them.

Sometimes the challenge is that both people are trying to make the other one break down first to admit love. Both are playing haughty, yet staying together, and it becomes a standoff—neither side will give in.

One very common reason that relationships end unhappily when they began with such sizzle is because the person who used haughtiness as a challenge to get attention, one day thinks that they've succeeded in getting the person into a relationship and now it's time to get their need to love someone back met.

So, they begin responding to the devotion of their RM

with equal ardor. This only confuses their RM, who suddenly doesn't know how to handle acceptance and love and doesn't have to prove him/herself anymore.

The challenge of haughtiness is gone, and disappointment turns to disinterest as the RM begins seeking someone else—and then ugly pain ensues.

You may think that, "Well, all I have to do is never to show that I care . . . just remain haughty-acting forever."

If so, then you remain cold-acting and suffer the sadness of unfulfillment. You would have to, because once you ever behaved in a warm way, the challenge would be gone and the game that held you together would be over.

Do you really want that?

Don't you deserve a real relationship where you are safe to be you? You may think that as long as you are marrying someone Rich, that you can act haughty until the day you die.

Maybe. But I doubt it. You see, one day, you are going to want to look a mate directly in the eyes and say, unashamedly, "I am absolutely crazy nuts about you" (or whatever words your passion designs).

You will want to *know* that the person is going to love you all the more for saying it—not suddenly feel the challenge is gone, and lose interest.

When I speak of Marriage to the Rich, I speak not just of Rich but also of Marriage. Marriage is the warm, cozy, soft pillow of your life, where you can rest your head safely.

What is the point of having money if you have no rest in your relationship? What's the point of having a relationship if you watch it being destroyed by lack of money?

You can be as lovable and as loving and adorable as you want to be and be worshiped for it, as long as you create a challenge in some other way.

A subtle challenge continues if your behavior contradicts your words. Perhaps you keep seeing other people. Perhaps you are more attentive to other people at times.

Just don't use coldness and haughtiness to create your challenge. It's self-defeating and love-defeating.

22

An RM's Domestic Staff, Employees, and Associates

> Money doesn't automatically create standards in an RM. You do.
>
> —Ginie Polo Sayles

Today's domestic staff in America represents a professional choice by individuals who are often better-educated than many of the people in the world.

Those who excel in a domestic staff are extremely proud of their profession. They execute their work with pride and satisfaction in expert services.

If you have come from a poor background and have not always understood domestic service, your first step is respect for each person and the duties they perform.

For both men and women, treat your RM's domestic staff and other employees in a friendly, interested manner. Ask how they're doing. Simply be one person saying something to another person.

However, never ask questions about your RM or about previous spouses or other people your RM may be dating. And don't mention anything personal about yourself.

Never confide anything about the RM or about your relationship with the RM.

Above all, don't act as if you are already lord or lady of the manor. Until you are, the employee probably has more influence than you do in many ways!

Be genuinely friendly but not familiar with your RM's domestic staff and employees. There are always two reasons for this rule:

197

1. It's not fair to the people who work for your RM.
2. It's not appropriate for you.

This same rule applies for your RM's office personnel, as well.

One woman used to take an RM's secretary to lunch. She thought she was being smart to become her buddy and to find out about him. Ha! The clever secretary not only enjoyed a free lunch, but she also planted the *wrong* information about the RM to misguide the dear lady who was paying for her lunch. The secretary, in the meantime, used information she, too, gleaned during those lunches to eventually win away her boss as her own RM!

AN RM'S ASSOCIATES AND FRIENDS

An RM will want you to be able to hold your own around the RM's friends or associates and around other people in general when you are together.

You will learn to be friendly, gracious, and not intimidated.

Be vibrant and sincere, keeping your subject matter to positive, happy subjects. Don't gush or over-compliment. Mostly listen and respond while you're learning.

Occasionally, you may encounter opposition. Someone who feels threatened by you may try to intimidate you with cool behavior, passive facial expressions, or eyes that stare or seem to check you out.

Such people are not worth very much, I assure you. Don't let them scare you. The problem is theirs, not yours. Be ready for them.

Don't behave defensively. Seem not to notice. If, however, you feel it is important to take a body-language stand in your own behalf, do so.

Look the person directly in the eye as if your vision goes right through them. Don't reflect that your eyes or face even register anyone being in the path of your vision. They don't exist.

Then, be the first to move your eyes away, as if you didn't see anything.

Don't jerk your eyes aside. That looks fearful. Instead, slide your eyes smoothly to one side. Fasten your attention on someone who is talking. Keep it there. Then, shift to turn your body so that your back is to the person who tried to intimidate you.

You don't want to make a habit of this look; but it can be helpful when someone is trying to intimidate you or to size you up negatively with your RM.

23

How to Handle
Trouble in RM City

Whoever gives the most, loves the most.

—Ginie Polo Sayles

How do you handle trouble in RM City?

IF YOU AREN'T LIVING TOGETHER

First, if things aren't moving along, cast doubt about *your* feelings for your RM. Express a vague discontent by being "unsure" of your feelings, without really doing anything major about it. Be a little distracted at times, but not depressed.

Pull something. Go out of town without saying so. Disappear. Don't answer your telephone for 24–48 hours and don't return calls for a while.

When you're back together, be more wonderful and happier than ever before. Have one or two moody, distracted moments. If your RM cares at all for you, this will create a little anxiety for your RM.

Don't pull this too often or it may lose its effectiveness.

IF YOU ARE LIVING TOGETHER

If you are living together and your RM was due home at, say, 6 PM but hasn't made it home by 9 PM, then *you* leave and stay gone all night.

Don't pack a bag, just take what you would normally have with you when you're out during the day. Then check

201

into a motel and do not telephone home. Do not. And do not park up the street, watching to see when your RM gets in.

Watch a movie in your motel room, go to the bar, talk on the telephone to someone your RM doesn't know and will never know, or anything to keep yourself from telephoning or going back.

Let the RM arrive home and discover you're not there.

Let your RM be the one to wait up for you, demanding where the hell you've been all night when you gently unlock the front door.

Don't acknowledge—ever—not ever in your entire life— that you waited for your RM . . . that you were ever aware that the RM was late.

Just swear you haven't been in bed with anyone (true). You got tied up earlier in the day ("Doing what?!?" Working . . . shopping . . ."), you had some drinks at Happy Hour, got to talking to a nice, interesting person you met there (don't give the name of a friend because that can be checked or betrayed) and the time got away.

You tried to call once but the line was busy (an obvious lie because your RM wasn't home). You felt you'd had too much to drink to drive home, so you stayed at a motel. You tried to call again when you got there and then fell asleep while waiting to call again.

Stick with that story until the day you die.

Never admit in a sentimental moment that you made it up as a ploy.

You may think you won't need future ploys and you probably won't, but you may, so don't confess. Add that you won't ever do it again.

In other words, whatever your RM intended to pull on you, catch it quickly and outwit your RM by making him or her think you're pulling it first.

Such situations are common between couples just before they give in and give up their truly single life-style and settle into something more committed.

It may not be these exact circumstances; but, usually,

there is some rebellious scene. The way you handle it will determine whether it is a final fling the RM has, or the beginning of a new trend that gradually means the end.

DESTRUCTIVE SCENARIO

If you, instead, wait at home until your RM shows up at 2 AM and either say nothing or create a scene of accusations, you have just positioned yourself as the victim, the loser. Your RM will then feel justified to begin pulling away and looking for an equal.

If, on the other hand, your RM's behavior backfires and you're the one who is not there when your RM gets home, you will have positioned your RM as the victim, the possible loser. Your RM will become more concerned with losing you and will straighten up and fly right.

Don't abase yourself by giving explanations, excuses, or long, drawn-out apologies.

Reinforce a strong self-image at all times. Be happy and warm, but withdraw your approval from time to time.

WITHDRAWING YOUR APPROVAL

Withdrawing your approval means not to say anything when your RM expects you to after the RM has expounded on a subject or shown you something.

Look at your RM, moving your eyes slowly from one eye to the other without a word, your face either passive or just slightly stern.

When you speak, change the subject.

If your RM presses back to the subject and asks what you think, look again with deliberation and say, "Oh, fine, fine," in such a way that the RM doesn't believe that's how you feel.

If your RM keeps saying, "You don't like it, do you?" say, "I gave you my answer. I have nothing more to say about it."

You should withdraw your approval at least once a week with a new RM to create curiosity and a need in the RM to win your approval.

For an RM you have been seeing for a while, don't withdraw your approval any more often than every two weeks to once a month—just to keep your RM from taking you for granted.

You can defeat yourself if you use it too often. People need more strokes than they do the frustration of withdrawn approval.

If frustration builds too much from not receiving more strokes than withdrawn approval, your RM *will* begin looking elsewhere for strokes and, I assure you, an RM can always get it—much to your loss.

Overused withdrawal of your approval can have the same unhappy effect of lower-class "haughtiness." Use sparingly.

EX-SPOUSES AND CHILDREN

Don't put up with ex-spouses.

Any ex-spouse who still calls for advice or comes over is infringing and has no rights to fairness or anything else— that's why he or she is an *ex*.

Be fair to your RM's children only to the extent that they do not interfere with your RM's relationship with you.

Children frequently compete with a new mate. Feeling threatened, they test their parent to see who means most to the parent.

When you and your RM discuss this, point out that psychology has shown that an adult's first responsibility is to his or her mate, not to a child. I must credit my husband, with his multiple family background, for having taught me this wise lesson.

If your RM is not this wise, you must be. Set this standard early in your relationship.

Once a child is made aware of the parent's relationship

priorities, the child will actually feel more secure. The child knows she or he is a child and that it is wrong to give them dominion and ''spouse-position priority.'' They feel more secure knowing the parameters.

A child may feel that because the child was born before the relationship with you was established, that the child is entitled to priority over you. Not true. One day, the child will be an adult and will fall in love and want to marry. If the parent does not like the person the child marries, is the child going to give the parent priority over the child's choice of a mate? No, of course not. Clearly, the child will not (and should not) give the parent a spouse-position priority in their lives. It is unhealthy for either parent or child to have precedence over the spouse.

Children need the ''tough love'' of ''No Trespassing'' signs in their parents' lives as much as they do tender love. A parent's primary adult relationship is a ''No Trespassing'' sign of foremost importance.

And any ex-spouse who questions the children about their visits, and expresses an opinion to the children about it, is vicariously continuing a relationship with the RM (although nobly masquerading as simply interested in the RM's welfare).

Be fair to **you**! Once sexual exclusivity is established, you owe your allegiance to each other first.

Once a relationship has developed that far, discuss the fact that you both owe your allegiance to each other over anyone else. You *must* clearly proclaim the superiority of your position. You *must*, or you'll lose your RM. You are not second place to someone's past or you don't have a future!

Don't accuse your RM of still caring for the ex-spouse and don't remind the RM of how badly the ex-spouse treated the RM. That gives the ex-spouse too much power.

When you speak of the ex-spouse at all, do so as if you consider the ex-spouse pitiful, pathetic . . . a loser . . . powerless . . . inferior. Remind your RM that if the divorce is final there is no reason for contact between the ex-spouse and the RM for advice or help. *Divorce means . . . "You're on your own!"* and husbandly or wifely duties end when living together ends.

PART IV

Marriage to the Rich

24

Marriage Strategies

> I don't think it's superior to marry for money and I don't think it's superior to marry for love. I think marriage is between two people, whatever their goals.
>
> —Ginie Polo Sayles

Now, let's turn our attention toward marriage so you can tie the knot with that seven-figure bank account.

What about love? I don't see how you can help loving anyone to some extent who is kind and generous to you. People are appalled when I say that. I am appalled that they can love someone who is mean and stingy—which is the opposite from kind and generous.

If your relationship has been consummated in bed before marriage, accelerate toward marriage.

In her book, *What Every Woman Should Know About Men*, Dr. Joyce Brothers has said that both sexes seek the positive qualities of their mothers. Both sexes. That means women seek husbands who have the positive qualities of their mothers, just as men seek wives who have the positive qualities of their mothers.

Find out what the positive qualities of their mothers were.

Then find out what some of the negative qualities of their mothers were. Usually, they still have feelings to resolve in what they perceived as negative qualities of their mothers, which showed up in their ex-spouse.

Know your RM's views of people living together before marriage. Also know if the RM has done so before. If so, the RM will do it again.

Know the RM's religious upbringing and views held about sex. Fundamentalist upbringing can create sexual conflicts of marrying someone they've "lived in sin" with. You may not want to live with an RM from this background before marriage.

Get a description of the RM's parents' relationship with each other. Was the RM's marriage in any way like that of the RM's parents?

The answers you receive from this query can give you an idea of your RM's marriage profile.

You can provoke the sensitive issues that surround the profile (Chapter 21) to get a response from your RM.

A ROMANTIC TEST TRIP

If beginning a sexual relationship before marriage is not a problem for you, and, your RM is sexually safe, then two months after you begin having sex together, suggest a trip together, if the RM does not.

This trip should not be a business trip but one entirely for pleasure. And it should provide at least three days together.

A trip that is burdened with business demands for you or for the RM doesn't provide the total focus on each other that deepens a relationship.

You become incidental to a business trip. You become a nice diversion, someone to talk to, a respite from the hollowness of traveling alone. That is not the stuff relationships are built on.

Yes, a few business trips together may be part of the beginning of your relationship with an RM; but, at some point, a trip for pleasure just for the two of you signals a more sincere interest, a better potential for something real developing.

LIVE TOGETHER

If the trip brings you *both* closer to each other, suggest living together for a short time.

Do this especially if you know that your RM lived with someone in the past whom he or she later married. If your RM simply has a history of living with people whom the RM did not marry, but did marry a person the RM did not live with, give it a lot of thought before deciding to.

If either of you have children living with you, you may not want to do this, depending on your personal view about it. Don't suggest living together if your preliminary questioning of your RM indicates your RM has an aversion to it.

If you opt to live together, specify that you would like to live together three months to see how compatible you are. Be sure to suggest a time frame.

It is best not to live together past six months to one year. It seems there is less chance of a marriage being successful the longer people live together *before* their marriage to each other.

Certainly, there are exceptions, but three months of living together is really the best. The glow is high.

You can even make it clear at the outset that you'd like to try living together for three months and that if it is a happy experience, you want to get married at that time.

If your RM agrees to live with you on those terms, all talk should be positive and glowing toward getting married.

One of the biggest mistakes you can make, though, is to become *too* reliable to anyone. That's why it's important to live together only long enough to intensify the relationship toward marriage.

If your RM has no hangups about living together before marriage and agrees to live with you, then your RM is desiring a closer relationship with you, too.

If your RM has no hangups about living together but

declines to live with you, then you are probably not going to marry that RM.

Yes, it could happen. For the time being, though, and for your own sake, try not to get even—put the RM on the back burner and get busy developing other relationships even if you don't want to. See more and more of other RMs and less and less of this one.

Taper off the sexual relationship and begin looking for someone else.

OTHER RMS

Never stop seeing and cultivating other RMs until you're married, whether you live together or not.

Naturally, for your sexual safety, you sleep with only one—the one you know will be monogamous; but, until you are actually married, it's foolish to burn bridges.

Stay in touch with all of them by telephone and for lunch. If your RM wants it stopped, state clearly that you won't do that until you feel able to really commit to someone.

It's better to keep the lines open with other RMs than to try to go out and start all over re-meeting RMs after a relationship with one has ended.

Besides, you are more attractive to other RMs when you are in the middle of a relationship with another one than you are to them when you are trying to get over one.

PRELIMINARY GUIDANCE

It's very important in your manner with your RM to have an attitude that *assumes* you and your RM *will* marry. Don't act as if you are afraid your RM won't marry you.

Once you and your RM begin living together, begin buying things jointly, investing jointly. Get your RM to let you use his or her credit cards.

If you are a woman, eventually get the RM to let you use

his name. These are good legal tools if your RM should ever try to take advantage of you or not do right by you.

During moments of uncertainty your RM may have about your relationship, *you* take control of it, saying cheerfully, "I'm not worried about us. You're mine and I know it. You're all mine."

Then turn the subject away as if you are truly unconcerned with losing the RM. Confident possessiveness is reassuring. It may take some practice, but it'll be worth it.

One of the most common mistakes made is to pretend not to want a relationship. If you want to be refreshingly different, be enthusiastic about love. If you've been married before, say you liked married life. But don't hint.

Say openly, happily, that relationships are healthy and you like being involved, you like it when you're in love.

Say you're glad to be normal and healthy and to enjoy something as natural as eventually getting married and creating a home with someone you love.

Instantly create a small challenge by adding that your only problem is that getting you to commit is a task cut out for someone special!

Once your RM says he or she loves you, *never* complain that the RM does not love you. Don't put the doubt in your RM's mind.

Don't ever criticize the relationship the two of you have together. Reinforce positives and happiness together. Tell your RM some compliments someone gave you about the two of you together as a couple. Another time, tell your RM compliments someone gave you about your effect on your RM's life.

And stay expensive. Ask for expensive items you see as if you expect them. Get money into you to increase your value to the RM more and more.

TACTICS

Confident Approach

1. Announce that you and your RM had better get started looking for a house if you're going to get married before the Christmas rush.

Some men and women have had success naming holiday periods for marriage because holidays revolve around home, family. That's why single people find themselves often feeling lonelier and depressed during holidays. Especially between Thanksgiving and Christmas.

Your RM may be more susceptible during that time because marriage seems warm, cozy, and comforting during those times. Weddings seem part of the celebration spirit and exchanging rings part of the gift-giving, exchanging vows, part of the spiritual momentum and sentimentality of the season.

2. Announce that you and your RM had better go ahead and file for your marriage license if you're going to get married by May (set 3 weeks to 2 months away at most).

If your RM is surprised, you respond by looking surprised at the RM, saying, "Well, it was your idea. You're the one who said we should get married in May."

If the RM denies it, insist that the RM is the one who wanted to get married in May. Add that actually, you had wanted to marry in early June, but the RM had been adamant about May.

If you want to, you can say the RM brought the subject up on an occasion when the RM had been drinking, but I think that's a weaker position. Tease your RM about having amnesia. Don't get heavy. Stay cheerful and see what happens. Always insist it was the RM's idea. Your RM should eventually believe you—seriously!

At least the subject has been introduced and you can gradually ingrain the idea into your RM a few days at a time and in a *non-pushy*, unworried manner. (*Never* confess.)

3. You can engineer a yes from your RM for marriage if you use a series of questions that automatically give the logical response of yes.

For instance: "Don't you think that if two people are sexually responsible and care about each other, that they should make love?" Your RM answers, "Yes."

You continue, "And don't you think that for the sake of sexual safety that they should make a commitment of monogamy?" Your RM answers, "Yes."

You close with, "Then, if they find themselves growing closer, don't you think it's natural that they get married?" If your RM says anything other than yes, if he says, "Not necessarily . . ." then you may want to re-evaluate what you expect from the relationship.

4. You can always be more forthright by taking your RM out for a special occasion or to a clever setting and propose in a cute, adorable way. Do this if you believe your RM really cares for you and only if you are willing to risk a "no" response.

Less Confident Approach

1. Once closeness and happiness are established through living together, if there has been no mention of marriage, then stage a "think-it-over" withdrawal.

Do not stage a think-it-over withdrawal until you know without a shadow of a doubt that you can keep yourself from giving in to gnawing insecurity, doubt, and raging fear. Then you are subject to making up an excuse to yourself and to him for calling or showing up or writing a letter.

Once you supposedly withdraw with a sense of independence and then give in to self-doubt, you will then be operating out of weakness, and any future "withdrawals" will not be taken seriously by your RM.

2. Erma Bombeck has a book entitled *Motherhood— Woman's Second Oldest Profession*. Motherhood is also woman's second oldest way of tying the knot—although I don't suggest you try that in the climate of our society today.

It might not work and then you could be making some tough decisions about abortion, single parenthood, or paternity suits! Not your ideal position to be in.

3. If, for some reason, during the year together, there has been resistance to getting married, issue an ultimatum and stick with it. You'll be glad later. Besides, you have been wise enough to still have other RMs waiting in the wings, haven't you?

Final Thoughts

However, if you and your RM have gotten this far, you will most likely get married and it will be a happy, romantic experience for both of you.

When you've successfully handled trouble in RM City and engineered a yes out of your RM, or your RM has proposed to you, make an agreement that the number-one priority between the two of you from now on will be your marriage to each other.

Once your RM agrees to that, take your marriage plans from the talk stage to the legal reality stage the very next day—blood test or marriage license, according to the requirements of your state.

If your RM protests the rush, point out that you have both agreed that your marriage to each other is the number-one priority to both of you and that this is proof that it is.

Don't Announce Anything to Anyone

Whatever month you suggest for marriage, be sure it's not more than two months away, preferably sooner. Beautiful weddings can be planned spontaneously within days and no one has time to get cold feet or interference from others.

Long, drawn-out affairs can terrify a male RM out of the whole thing. Sudden excitement is more romantic. If the RM wants a small, quiet wedding, do it! You can always have elaborate anniversary parties. It's more important to make it special for the two of you than for a lot of other people!

Impress others with the fact that you actually married the RM, not with a wedding, if there has to be a choice.

ISOLATE YOUR RELATIONSHIP

Whether or not you and your RM live together first, spend most of your time alone together, just the two of you. You might *occasionally* meet a dating couple or happily married couple for some event, but it's best not to get involved on a regular basis with each other's friends. Large group parties are the exception.

I know this sounds radical, but I even suggest you avoid meeting each other's parents, children, best friends, bosses, or coworkers until *after* you're married.

Marriage is between *two* people. There are those who will tell you that you marry each other's family and friends. That is not true unless you *let it* be true.

Even close relatives are outsiders. Your parents are outsiders. Your children are outsiders . . . unless you are foolish enough to let them become involved.

They can't always see what you see in someone—and they may secretly fear losing their influence over you even if they sound as if they're only concerned for your good.

This is your life and no one knows more about your needs and your good than you.

Their opinions could end the chances of marriage for you—a marriage that could be your greatest source of strength and happiness in the long run.

One of my students, a lovely 46-year-old widow, met a fabulous RM who wanted to marry her. She was thrilled; but after he met her 80-year-old mother, who ridiculed him to her, she broke up with him. Her mother died a few years later and he, in the meantime, had married and was living in Europe for a while. She was alone.

She said to me, "My mother was afraid of losing me to him. She'd had me all to herself since my husband died. I guess she thought I wouldn't take care of her, which is ridiculous. She ruined him for me. I never liked displeasing my mother. Now, I wish I had."

The stirring truth is that children grow up and lead their own lives. Parents grow old and die. Friends move away.

No. Don't involve any of them in your romantic life. Once you're married, they'll have to accept your spouse.

If you move straight into the marriage without mentioning it to other people until afterward, you might also be lucky enough to get your RM to the altar before anyone has time to think of (or be reminded of) a Prenuptial Agreement. An RM who would be inclined to have a Prenuptial Agreement probably will think of it, but . . . maybe not.

25

Prenuptial Agreements

Prenuptial Agreements are only as good or as bad as the person making them. Be sure it's not financially a parent-child Agreement that ends up being a persecutor-victim Agreement.

—Ginie Polo Sayles

Even a will is created because death is considered inevitable. The same feeling can surround creating a Prenuptial Agreement, which is a plan for the *end* of a marriage.

However, there are people who have lasting marriages built around a Prenuptial Agreement.

Don't be afraid of the words. Prenuptial Agreements are only as good or as bad as the person who makes them. The situation may justify it: exorbitant prior debts or other difficulties of one spouse that would be unfair to thrust on the new, loving spouse. No matter what state you live in, Prenuptial Agreements are legal. The court in your state can rule on those that are contested. And if you have no Prenuptial Agreement, your marriage is subject to the laws of your state.

A Prenuptial Agreement may be overruled on charges of:

1. Duress.
   Your RM gives you a Prenuptial Agreement to sign while wedding guests are listening to "O Promise Me," while waiting for you and the groom to arrive at the altar.
2. Unfairness.
   Clearly, one person is getting disproportionately more than the other.

3. Misrepresentation.
   One mate did not fully reveal assets and financial
   position.
4. Fraud.
   An attempt to defraud the other.

WHAT TO DO

There is just no substitute for having a lawyer represent
you if you are presented with a Prenuptial Agreement.

If by the day of your wedding you have not been
presented with a Prenuptial Agreement, don't take anything
for granted.

In my classes, I jokingly say, "Invite a good contract
attorney to be your guest at the wedding . . . just in case
you have to ask, 'Is there a lawyer in the house?' " The truth
is, I'm serious. Do it.

If you are confronted with a Prenuptial Agreement well in
advance of the wedding, tell your RM that since this has
been drawn up by the RM's lawyer, you would like the RM
to pay for the attorney of your choice to look at it. Do not
reveal the name of the attorney of your choice. Just say that
you haven't decided on your attorney yet but that you will
let the RM know how much to deposit in your account after
you have located one and gotten estimates of cost.

If your RM will not pay and you cannot afford an
attorney, telephone your county, borough, or parish and find
out where free legal aid is provided.

Law schools usually have intern programs for students
who are close to graduating from law school. Telephone to
see if you qualify for help. You must have some assistance
in the matter.

If an RM is not going to pay for you to have legal
assistance, chances are you are getting into a really bad deal.

THE UNDERLYING PSYCHOLOGY
OF A PRENUPTIAL AGREEMENT

Know the underlying psychology of an unfair Prenuptial Agreement.

Most people talk in noble terms of fairness. Rarely is that the motive. Selfishness, fear, cruelty are too often hidden in the talk of fairness.

In the case of duress, an RM is using embarrassment as a weapon against you to force you, to manipulate you to agree to the RM's terms.

It is easy to see that an RM who puts you into this situation or who insists on an unfair Prenuptial Agreement is attempting to create a parent-child dependency in the relationship. There may be a deep-seated fear within the RM that the only way to keep you is to control the purse strings.

That may sound flattering at the outset, but it is really a persecutor/victim relationship. Helplessness is not attractive and I doubt you'll keep your RM's interest very long with such an arrangement.

You'll be taking your chances by signing an Agreement you do not truly agree with, but the hope is that if your marriage collapses, the court will consider it signed under duress.

Be aware of the fact that the RM took advantage of you during your glow of desire to get married by slipping you an unfair document.

Now, you must take advantage of the RM during the afterglow of marriage itself, which exists during the first 18 months of marriage.

Rather than leave yourself unprotected in this situation, if you go through with the marriage, at least research the countries that have secret bank accounts. Begin socking away whatever cash and gifts you can charm your RM into giving you so that you never tolerate abuse or fear.

Discreetly find out from your new set of Rich friends who

the best attorneys are who handle Prenuptial Agreements and visit one of the attorneys when the time comes. And in those cases, it most likely will come.

SELF-ESTEEM AND PRENUPTIAL AGREEMENTS

If, however, you work constantly on your self-esteem through positive self-reprogramming statements, visualization, accepting responsibility for your life, and creating the life you desire by taking risks, I don't believe you'll ever find yourself faced with an unhappy Prenuptial Agreement.

The very Richness of your being will overflow into the life around you and pull to you only the best.

And even if you were presented with one, your self-esteem would be so high that you could make demands in your own behalf and, if they weren't received, you could walk away from it without batting an eye.

26

Who Marries the Rich?

The Rich are going to marry somebody. Why not you?

—GINIE POLO SAYLES

"I may commit many follies in life, but I'll never marry for love." Those were the words of Benjamin Disraeli, as quoted by Dale Carnegie in his book, *How to Win Friends and Influence People*. Benjamin Disraeli was a 19th-century Prime Minister of England.

Disraeli kept his word. Brought up with money and successful, himself, as a writer, he nevertheless was rumored to have had bad loans. He married a woman close to fifteen years older than he and for her money and position.

It was—surprise—one of the happiest marriages in history. So, you are in good company with high achievers. After all, the Prime Minister of England was a Gold Digger!

People don't like to admit that Gold Diggers/Mercenaries often have a happy marriage and create interesting history—but history is on your side.

HUMOR

Like Disraeli, it helps to have a sense of humor about your very serious pursuit of an RM. Some lighthearted Gold Digger quips keep you from having a brittle attitude that doesn't attract anybody, much less an RM.

In the stock market, there is the advice to "Buy low, sell high" for making money. You can say, "Marry low, divorce high!"

Any goal you pursue with a sense of humor as well as a strong sense of purpose is, somehow, easier to achieve.

FOUR TYPES WHO SEEK RICH MATES

There are basically four types of people who want to marry the Rich:

1. Men and women who have money themselves from a previous marriage or family background and who want a mate from their own social and financial stratum.
2. Men and women who want a Rich Mate to bankroll their own careers or simply to upgrade their standard of living if they have no career.
3. Men and women with a basic self-confidence that they can make a Rich Mate happy and have a desire to do so.
4. Men and women who have emerged from a previous wasted relationship of humiliating poverty with a mate who wouldn't work or who used them, and now they feel a bit "had."

All these types can be successful, of course; however, the people who have the last motive—those who have come out of bitter marriages of hardship with someone who wouldn't work or who exploited them—these people stand the greatest chance of marrying the Rich.

Why? Because they are ready to be on the taking end of a relationship for a change and they will give only what will be appreciated.

They are unwilling to put up with anything but the best financial treatment from now on because they understand, bitterly, the dynamics of sex, love, and money.

27

The Power of Desire

You will only rise as high as your comfort-level.
Desire is the key to raising your comfort-level.

—Ginie Polo Sayles

Don't worry, you already have what it takes to Marry the Rich. And that is your **Desire System**.

Your Desire System is the most important key to Marrying the Rich. Your Desire System is the engine that runs the entire process of achieving goals.

All you have to do is to feed your Desire System, nurture your Desire System, cherish and cultivate your Desire System, until it controls you, until it motivates everything you do, every choice you make on the tiniest level.

How do you cultivate and nurture your Desire System? Through a method I call "Desire Shopping."

1. Make a list of all the places in your city that are known for their opulence where you can go for little or no money:

(a) The most expensive clothing stores.
(b) Fine furniture stores.
(c) Interior design shops.
(d) Art galleries.
(e) Sumptuous hotel lobbies.
(f) Gift shops.
(g) Fine international department store chains that are known for their excellence.
(h) Expensive boutiques that cater to money.
(i) Historical mansion tours.
(j) Quality antique shops (not the kind that just sell used furniture).

   (k) Estate auctions.

   (l) Shopping centers that cater to the Rich. In cities, they are usually near or in the wealthy neighborhoods.

2. Go there to acquaint yourself with the finest. You want to get used to having your body near the very best that money can buy.

3. While there, observe details. Note how these places are different from the ordinary. Notice lights, sights, sounds, scents, textures, combinations, and how each works together into quality craftsmanship and elegant detail.

4. Gather samples of the costliest perfumes and fragrances in the world. Study foods and coffees sold in the gourmet sections.

5. It is especially important to go anywhere that intimidates you. You are only intimidated because you are not familiar with this type of backdrop for your daily life.

By going to these places every day for 60 to 90 days, you will become increasingly comfortable.

Intimidation will fade as you gradually realize that all expensive objects in all luxurious places are inferior to *you*, no matter what they cost. They are a backdrop that enriches life for you.

6. You now respect objects for their craftsmanship, not their cost. You refine your taste and learn to appreciate craftsmanship by touring museums and historical mansions.

7. If you see ads in magazines or newspapers for fine estate auctions, order brochures and study them. Go, if you can.

8. Study magazines such as *The Robb Report, Architectural Digest, Town and Country*, and *Gourmet*.

9. Go through the Yellow Pages of your telephone directory and get your name on the mailing lists of major art galleries, and on every association and organization that depends on donors/founders, such as many fine arts or performing arts groups.

You will find yourself yearning for many of the items you

see while Desire Shopping . . . yearning for a life-style that includes these luxuries.

Be glad. Be glad when you feel the intense, frustrated, unhappy yearnings. It means your Desire System is getting healthier, stronger.

Your Desire System is making you uncomfortable with your present condition. Your Desire System is insisting that you change your life in whatever way you *have to*, in order to have what you want.

The purposes of Desire Shopping include:

1. To learn to be comfortable in the most expensive surroundings.
2. To not let people who work in these places intimidate you.
3. To learn not to be intimidated by the cost and quality of luxury, because all luxurious objects are inferior to you.
4. To develop your self-esteem by treating yourself better than you do anyone else.
5. To fine-tune your taste to a discriminating awareness.
6. Most important of all, to whet your appetite for the finest until your Desire System consumes you and demands it. And then . . . you can get it.

28

When You Should
Not Marry Rich

Millionaires need love, too!

—GINIE POLO SAYLES

The purpose of my book is to provide information so that if you do not marry the Rich, it won't be because you don't qualify or don't know how. It will be your option.

You may decide that even though you now qualify as marriageable for a Rich Mate, there may be equally important reasons *not* to marry someone Rich.

There are ten major reasons you may be reluctant to marry an RM. Five of those reasons I consider to be excellent reasons not to marry Rich; whereas five of them I consider less significant, but important only if they are important to you.

EXCELLENT REASONS TO NOT MARRY AN RM

Reason Number 1: Abuse/Fear

Certainly, you will never find marriage to the Rich worthwhile if you must tolerate abuse or abase yourself in order to maintain the marriage.

I must add at this point, though, that there are individuals who have done just that, and then, after a divorce, they have made money writing a book or selling movie rights about it.

229

Reason Number 2: Is It Worth It?

In some cases, it takes no special skills to marry an RM, only a compliant willingness to do anything the RM says.

I am reminded of such a case, when a woman married a wealthy heir by providing an offer he couldn't refuse—no financial demands and total sexual obedience—which not only created their marriage but later destroyed it.

As I pointed out in Chapter 15, you may be able to marry an RM who can only be authoritarian with people who are not in the RM's social class.

But what is the good of being married to the Rich if you received only a one-thousand-dollar-a-month allowance from a 25-million-dollar husband, had to serve cocaine at parties, and had to bring an extra woman to bed with you in order to please your husband sexually? And finally, if, in divorce, you lose your children and subject them to scandal?

RMs are no different from anyone else. If they have trouble with sexual satisfaction or being looked up to, they will marry someone who is financially and sexually an easy mark. Do you want to be that someone who is willing to be "used" without complaint?

If there is one thing that I want for you it is that you love the Rich and win—that you maintain control of your happiness within the marriage relationship to the Rich—that you are an asset treated with honor.

And yet, the tormented marriage was still worth it to the woman in the long run. Her life continues to revolve around being his ex-wife. Her name is known for no other reason than to have married him and told all. In fact, the former marriage is still her bread and butter, both financially and socially. It has become her identity.

So even a "poor" Rich marriage can end up being worth it in some ways.

Tattletale fame is nothing new. But, it doesn't have to be that way. You can marry an RM and use the position in positive ways to get an education, a higher degree, launch a business, a talent or design, a career, or a shining social reputation.

If marriage to an RM stipulates little money to you and compliance to the RM, I won't tell you not to go ahead. I will warn you that it probably won't last.

But, ultimately, it's you who must decide if you are willing to endure it and if you can leverage it to your advantage. Determine for yourself if the marriage requirements will be worth it.

Reason Number 3: Your Own Fulfillment

After three years of steadfastly pursuing your Marry Rich goals, I suggest you take honest inventory of your life.

1. Are you still ending up with Saccharine Daddies or Mommas?
2. Are you using Marry Rich goals as a means of avoiding relationships with real marriage potential, yet are not any closer to a real relationship with RMs?
3. Have you gotten hooked on a certain RM and nothing is moving any closer to marriage than it was two years ago?

Marriage to the Rich is intended as a personal fulfillment of goals you have for yourself. However, if marriage to the Rich has become a pursuit that allows you to postpone fulfillment, then it is no longer a healthy goal.

You will know that is the case if you find that you are still involved with unsatisfying RMs, or RMs with no marriage potential. Marry a mate with Rich potential instead, and you can still achieve your goal.

Reason Number 4: Posterity

If you are over thirty-five years old and you have never been married, have never had children, and want children—

plus, the RMs in your life are not coming across for you, begin to include the "Future RMs" I will describe, later, into your love life and consider them marriageable.

You have a biological clock as well as achievements to consider, if you're a woman—and achievements to consider, if you're a man.

Reason Number 5: Loneliness

No matter what age you are, listen to the winds of loneliness in your own heart. Loneliness is inevitable at times, no matter whom you want to marry. But, if loneliness becomes an overwhelming facor, it may be better to marry someone with potential and direct your energies together for achievement.

MARGINAL REASONS NOT TO MARRY AN RM

Reason Number 6: Money Is Transitory

There is the possibility that your RM can lose money. After all, there is no guarantee that an RM you marry will stay Rich. If it bothers you that money is transitory and it can be gone very quickly, you may want to consider marriage alternatives.

If this should happen to your RM, my personal feeling is that you never abandon an RM who has defended you with his dollar and his name.

Mercenary though you are—and I hope you are—you see the RM through the crises. Afterward, you can leave if you want to and you will be admired by other RMs who witnessed the fine caliber of your strength. This will enhance your opportunities with other RMs for marriage.

Reason Number 7: It's Not Your Money

Another consideration is that even though you Marry Rich, that doesn't make *you* Rich. You are the spouse of someone Rich. In some cases, if you are ambitious, it can help you. I, personally, am not Rich; and Reed and I have separate businesses, although we sometimes do similar work. But a mate with money often understands your goals.

Still and all, it's not your money. So, if it bothers you to think that your mate will be the one with the money and not you, then you may want to consider marriage alternatives.

Reason Number 8: Love Is Your Hot Button

Go ahead and marry for love the first time you marry. If it lasts, I applaud you.

If, however, you have been married before or if money is very important to you, yet love is still important to you, consider the following.

Love—or the magical effects of love—can thin somewhat after three or four years. Many men and women who cheat begin cheating after three or four years in their marriages of "love." And a lot of marriages end after a few years.

Too, I urge you to consider that love—a wonderful love—so often develops after marriage to someone who is kind and generous with you. Remember, Millionaires need love, too!

I knew of a woman who suffered through four years of a love affair with a married man. "Love" was the reason she stayed in it.

During the fourth year, a man she met at a party in another town asked if he could take her to dinner when he had business in her city.

She agreed and went to dinner with him a few times, always thinking about her married lover throughout the entire meal. She never gave the man a second thought after her dates with him.

As the fourth year closed, she decided to take a job in another city, in hopes of forcing her lover to his senses so he would leave his wife and marry her.

She found the job, gave notice at her current job, gave notice on her apartment, broke the news to her lover, and packed her belongings in boxes, waiting for him to call or come over and plead with her not to leave.

On the day she was to move out, she realized her lover was not going to insist she stay, nor was he going to leave his wife for her.

She also realized she didn't want to move or to start a new job. She telephoned her new employers in the other city and told them she wasn't coming. She telephoned her old job but they had replaced her. She telephoned her landlord, but her apartment had already been leased.

She sat down on the packed boxes, feeling depression settle over her. Her telephone rang. She jumped to answer it only to find it was the boring man from out of town, wanting to take her to dinner.

"Sorry," she said, "this is not a good time."

"May I come by to see you?" he asked.

"This is really not a good time," she repeated, dismally.

"I promise, I won't stay but five minutes," he insisted. Finally, she agreed on those terms. When he arrived, he took one look at the boxes and asked what she was doing.

"I don't know," she said. "I don't have a job and I don't have a place to live. I don't know what I'm going to do."

He brightened. "Well, the reason I wanted to see you tonight is because I thought you might like to marry me."

Shocked, she turned to look at him.

Her lover, whom she ached with longing to marry, hadn't called. And there he stood—a man who was everything she *never* wanted—asking her to marry him.

She was just about to open her mouth to say "No" when the words "Give him a chance" went through her mind.

Instead, she said, "Yes." (That's more than a "chance"!)

In three weeks they were married and moved to his house in another town. She couldn't believe her eyes when she saw it. The house was a beautiful, large three-story house of dramatic design.

A year later, she was driving her luxury car, when she was overcome by a longing to see or talk to her former lover. She pulled the car to the side of the street and began crying.

To her surprise, the memories of this past year with her kind, generous husband began flowing like a healing balm through the memories of anguish from the married lover who was too mean and stingy with his love to be faithful to either his wife or her and too mean and stingy with his money to indulge either with more than token gifts.

She stopped crying. Her thoughts swam with the proof of love her husband had given her. His interest in her welfare surrounded her and clothed her. His delight in giving her gifts and his interest in her happiness filled her heart with warmth. And she realized how happy she was with him, how much she . . . loved . . . him.

She had fallen in love with her husband *after* they married. She truly loved him.

Love doesn't have to precede marriage. Love can be a choice. Love does grow and develop as you become attached to the kindness and consideration of a person.

But, if you consider it noble to marry for love, even if it is someone who is mean and stingy with you, then marrying for money is something you might never find satisfying anyway.

Certainly, an affair with someone mean and stingy while married to someone kind and generous is my final compromise to you. But, if you must marry the boor, then, of course, I offer you my very best condolences, er, wishes.

I hope, if you marry for love, it will at least be a person who is Rich in spirit with you! That is understandable!

Reason Number 9: The Sex Is So-o-o Good

Virtually all tests that have ever been conducted indicate that sex slips in priority after the first eighteen months of marriage—and usually ends up on a slower track over time than most couples will ever admit.

Sex is usually important for marrying the Rich; however, if it slips after eighteen months and you must have steamy sex, remember, it might stay steamier with a lover as long as you have a nice Porsche to ease into after lovemaking and a sweet, gentle RM to welcome you home.

However, if you must, must, must have a sex machine as your lawful, wedded, for however long it lasts—go for it!

Reason Number 10: Same Age and Background

Many people want someone who is in their same age category or who shares a similar background. There is no denying this can be attractive.

The warning here, though, especially for ambitious women, is that a man who is in your same age category and who shares your background of lacking wherewithal, may have too much in common with you.

In fact, I have found that men and women who are ambitious and who are at the same starting point on the totem pole end up having more relationship problems than just about any other combination. This is because ambitious people need someone to nurture them in their achievements.

You may each feel you can do that for each other—and sometimes you can. But sometimes, when both your careers are in a crunch of growth, you don't have it to give each other, although you want to. This means that neither of you is getting what is needed from the relationship at that time.

Another difficulty is that whereas you both want to see each other succeed, one of you can begin to feel a little like a failure when the other begins succeeding more. There may be denial about this, but an insidious competition enters the relationship and tiny resentments mixed with pride for each other.

Finally, there also is the issue of no one having made it to the point of really being able to help the other construc- tively. You are facing a lot of the same problems for the first time. Of course, it can work, if you both stay aware of it, but it can be very difficult.

If you marry someone who is of a different age and who has a background of wealth, you receive advice and help with perspective.

Too, the RM already has a financial identity established and will not be in competition with you, and will normally be intrigued with helping you and watching you succeed.

CONSIDERING "FUTURE RMS"

Whether you have excellent reasons not to marry an RM or marginal reasons for not marrying an RM, you may want to consider those women and men who have the ability to become Rich Mates in the future.

If you are both patient and ambitious, there are guidelines to follow for you to determine if someone may be a Future RM.

If you do widen your scope to include Future RMs, then look for someone: (1) Who has earning potential; (2) who has been rich before; or (3) who is almost rich.

It could just be that you are the missing "Success Factor" to transform this person's life from "almost" to "actuality"!

The following types of Future RMs may make your life emotionally Richer in the *now* and financially Richer in the future.

MR./MS. NOT QUITE RICH

This can be a good choice because the person has had enough drive and personal achievement to make significant success happen in his/her life.

Be sure the person is not too, too self-satisfied about his/her achievements in life and is content and resistant to higher levels of money goals.

MR./MS. HAS-BEEN RICH

Potential has been tried-and-true here. This is a person who either has connections—if the money lost was inherited; or the person knows how to make the money again—if the money lost was earned.

When you consider a Has-Been Rich for marriage, determine if the person lost money due to reasons of the economy or due to personal weaknesses that sabotaged his/her success.

If it's a matter of the economy, this person has all the potential in the world to remake a fortune. It was not his/her fault in full.

Another benefit of marrying a Has-Been Rich is if you are very ambitious for your own creative projects or business ventures.

The Has-Been Rich may very well be looking around for a new start in life and a new direction to translate his/her business experience and acumen into. This means you will benefit from tremendous previous but proven success patterns of your partner.

If the person has self-sabotaged, there is still hope as long as you take sufficient steps to protect yourself and your business from it. This person is a wealth of information and connections that can help you succeed.

MR./MS. POTENTIAL

Everyone always plans to be rich one day. On the day of my own dear father's retirement from civil service work, he was sixty-eight years old and he looked at me and said, "You know, I always intended to get rich . . . but, somehow . . . the time got away from me."

I've never forgotten that and I appreciate his having shared it with me. It gave me a value and perspective of time and achievement. The following question can help you discern if there is any probability at all of it happening.

1. How often does the person switch his/her goal as to what the person wants to achieve?

Most people with potential are fairly single-minded. They don't think they want to be a lawyer one day and a doctor the next. Yes, they may change their minds or direction, but it is not a fluctuating state of mind.

2. Does the person have any credits of achievement? Has the person followed through on any goal?

3. What is the person doing *now* toward achieving his/her "be rich" goal?

In other words, if she says she's going to make a fortune as a rock star, but she can't carry a tune and isn't even taking singing lessons, I think you might want to consider the disparity of *when* she plans to begin becoming a rich rock star.

Alternatives

There, that gives you some alternatives to cold-blooded, bloodthirsty gold-digging that can still translate into success and wealth for you in the long term.

If anyone says, "Well, I saw you reading the *Marry Rich*

book. What would Ginie Polo Sayles say to you about marrying someone without money?''

Look them in the eye and say, ''Are you kidding? Ginie gave me her blessing!''

Your happiness. Your choices. That's what this book is ultimately about. Bless you!

29

Having Inner Richness

> When I speak of Marriage to the Rich, I speak not just of Rich but also of Marriage. Marriage is the warm, cozy, soft pillow of your life, where you can rest your head safely.
>
> —GINIE POLO SAYLES

You hear a lot about Inner Richness. I know it sounds cliché, but I've learned that clichés are clichés for a reason—they're true.

If it is true that we attract to us our own level of thought and values, then the foundation for marrying the Rich is to restructure our thoughts and values.

Inner Richness is a developed state of mind that expresses itself in your personality with people.

I don't try to explain how these principles work. I think that is presumptuous of anyone to fully know how Life operates. I only know that it does work.

Inner Richness is not just a sweet way of thinking. Inner Richness boils down to three specific "acts."

Those three acts include:

FAITH

This can be a confusing term. Faith is not just something that you have in your mind saying, "Oh, I believe . . ." and then doing nothing.

No, indeed. If you really have *faith*, you will realize that *faith is an act of risk*.

Let's look at the double-faceted quality of faith.

(a) Faith is an act.
(b) Faith is a risk.

Faith Is an Act

The best example I can think of is a farmer. A farmer goes out into a barren field with nothing but teeny, tiny seeds that bear no resemblance to the wheat or corn he wants to see waving in the now barren field.

Yet, he goes out, day after day, and works hard plowing and planting the tiny seed into the empty field.

Why?

Because he *believes*. He believes that if he plows the field and plants the seed and tends it that the field will in time be converted into waves and waves of beautiful wheat, instead of a barren field.

Faith is an act. If you believe something will happen, you act on it.

The farmer would not work this way if he didn't *believe* it would work.

If the farmer simply said, "Oh, I believe that wheat will grow on my fields," but did nothing, he would be very disappointed.

Faith is an act, not just a mental state of mind. If you really *believe* something will happen, you act on it.

Faith Is Risk

If there is no possibility of loss, then faith isn't required. No, the double-faceted quality of faith requires that you face opposition—and sometimes, even that you fail.

The farmer may stand in heartbreak and watch his crops ravaged by hail or flood or drought.

There is no denying the pain you risk.

But, faith is an act that, although the person may fail many times, he experiences the pain, assesses what he can do to minimize loss and then goes for winning again!

And failure is just a word. It is just a part of the Learning Process that helps you accumulate information until you know how to do something the best way possible.

Realize, too, though, that in the face of failure, faith still believes it can be done—and acts on it until it *is* done.

GIVING

Giving is an act.

What you give are resources of your personality, not money, until you have money to give. Yes, if you can anonymously help someone financially and never tell anyone you did it, then do so.

But give, give, give a loving nature and vibrant happiness to all the happiness-starved, attention-starved people everywhere you go.

I'm not talking about just giving to the poor. I'm talking about giving cheerful attention to the business executives, their secretaries, the cashier, your best friend, a neighborhood pet, an elderly shopper, a child tagging along with his parents.

If you become really aware of people everywhere you go and respond cheerfully to their existence without lingering, you can't imagine how much magnetism you will begin generating.

Realize that although you are interested in marrying money, it's not because you consider a person who has money as superior to anyone else.

Of course not. You consider all people as precious. You may not date someone without money but only because you know you would not be happy together—"Be ye not unequally yoked togeth·.r"—not because you consider any less of the person.

Give kindness and appreciation to people as much as possible. It isn't always possible because you are human. But really try to be loving.

One mental trick I perform a lot is that when I pass

someone on the street whose life seems to be in the pain of waste, I look the person in the face and say in my mind, "I am you and you are me." Do this with successful people as well so that you see there is no line of demarcation on the human soul.

Many times I've seen my dreams fulfilled shortly after an act of giving. Once, I longed for a particular opportunity. Realizing how limited and hopeless my chances were, my mind also wandered to older people and how limited and hopeless their lives can feel.

I thought of my elderly aunts whom I hadn't seen in years and wrote each one a letter, telling them how much what they had given me as a child meant in my life.

Within hours of that act, a door of opportunity suddenly opened for me in a strange way and my opportunity was fulfilled.

Give your encouragement and vibrance and *go*. Make no claim upon the person's time. Seek nothing back. Let them enjoy it without feeling imposed upon.

Give vibrance without lingering. Give it. Give, give, give.

FORGIVING

Forgiveness is an act.

Forgiveness is not a mental process of just saying, "I forgive so-and-so." No, that's too easy and it doesn't work.

Believe me, you will want to learn and to utilize this tremendous power of forgiveness, because it can move your life forward in giant leaps.

Every time my life has been stuck, if I sat down and said to myself, "Okay, who is it that I need to release from the bondage of my emotions and thoughts?" I always came up with a person or persons.

At that point, I wrote out brief notes of encouragement to that person (I write brief notes of encouragement to people, anyway, that have nothing to do with forgiveness) and in the note, *I never mentioned the problem between us.*

As long as the problem is even mentioned, it has power. As long as the problem is even mentioned, it cancels the forgiveness.

Then I mailed the brief note without a return address. A return address invites a response. As long as you are wanting a reaction from the person, that's not releasing them. By wanting a response from them you are still tying them into your feelings.

Once mailed, I never followed up, never tried to reinstate the relationship—because you can be setting yourself up for another problem if you do so. I simply put it to rest forever by releasing them and leaving it forever.

Often, within hours or a few days, my life leaped forward in amazing ways.

Somehow—and I don't claim to know how—our acts of faith, giving, and forgiving are the doors of opportunity and fulfillment to what we wish to create of our lives.

If we are facing blockages, they may be blockages of our own emotions, our own limited view of our world. Pettiness keeps you trapped in a small world. I have seldom seen petty people succeed.

I confess that I cannot always forgive someone immediately. It may take days, weeks, months, even a year or so in some cases.

But I have found that once I do it, I wish I could have done it sooner. The benefits are far, far greater than the wound, even though I may have been right in the situation.

CHANGE WHAT YOU SAY

What if you don't have faith? What if you try and try and try to believe something will happen for you, but you still feel as if you're lying to yourself and you're afraid it won't happen?

Well, one thought process is canceling out the other so that you are immobilized—unable to act—and nothing changes in your life.

But, don't worry. Faith can be developed.

How? Faith comes by hearing; therefore, you must guard your words carefully so that what you hear yourself saying is what you want to believe and what you want to happen.

Words are powerful and they can create the world you live in. Words are keys that unlock doors. Words start wars and words end them.

Begin to heal and redirect your life by choosing your words about yourself and about your life as carefully as you can.

Now, don't become obsessively superstitious about them, because we are human beings and we will occasionally say things without thinking or that do not reflect what we meant.

But, by and large, your words are the single most important ally that you have in reaching your goals.

Affirmations are used by many people today. I am no exception. I found that when I began using affirmations, my world changed. I still use affirmations for specific goals I work toward.

You are supposed to say an affirmation 21 times in a row for 21 days for maximum effectiveness and then follow up often thereafter.

The first time I said my affirmations, I was halfway into it, when I stopped and said to myself, "I'm lying! I don't feel the way these affirmations say I feel."

I have never been able to lie to myself, so I stopped saying the affirmations for several days.

Suddenly, it hit me—Wait a minute—a statement is a lie only if it is something that has already happened in the past and you are saying it is different from the way it happened.

But an affirmation states the present and the present is in progress and hasn't happened yet. That means you can stop whatever is in progress and decide to change course—which means to reprogram whatever is in progress.

I can *choose* to feel—right now—the way the affirmation states that I feel. It states that I feel that way in the present and I can choose to do that right now.

Immediately, I returned to saying my affirmations and I did so with great emotion, vigor, and allowed myself to not *hope to feel*, but to actually let myself *know the feeling*. Once I knew it wasn't a lie, I knew it was a possibility. It could be real and I chose to open myself to the desires of my heart really happening.

Why 21 Times for 21 Days?

There's no hocus-pocus in it. Very simply, it has been shown that a human being takes about 3 weeks (which is 21 days) to form a new habit.

Also, it takes repetition of up to about 21 times to correct a practiced habit—a mistake in playing a musical instrument, say.

So you combine the repetition of correcting what you say to yourself and do so daily for 3 weeks and your thinking takes on a new habit—you have reprogrammed yourself.

Once you have done this, you have also programmed faith—and because faith is an act, you will begin to act in accordance with it.

Faith comes by hearing. Choose what you want to believe and then let yourself hear it over and over until faith takes hold and you will know when that happens because you will begin to act accordingly. You will act as if you believe it because you *will* believe it.

We are going to be thinking thoughts all day long, anyway, so why not choose the thoughts we want to have about the things we want to have happen?

My faith took hold very quickly and results began flowing in before the 3 weeks were ended.

POSITIVE SELF-REPROGRAMMING STATEMENTS

Priority Affirmations

For preliminary mental and emotional cleansing, so nothing impedes you, straighten your priorities by stating each of the four following Priority Affirmations 3 consecutive times before stating your Goal Affirmations.

I, [your name] _____ , readily accept responsibility for all my relationships—past, present, and future—with the opposite sex. I alone am responsible for the choices I make that allow relationships into my life.

I, _____ , maintain personal safety as my first priority in developing relationships. Personal safety includes a sensible awareness of physical and mental safety in forming relationships.

I, _____ , now unbind and release from my soul, all binding unforgiveness from *[name the situation or person]*. I set you free from the bondage of my emotions and my thoughts and truly wish you happiness and joy in the grace of God forever. (If several people or situations, say it 3 times per individual.)

I, _____ , now give into the universe and know that I, too, shall be given unto. I give radiant joy, sparkling humor, and a wealth of enthusiasm to everyone whose life touches mine. I receive and welcome back into me the inflow of love and richness that is mine by divine law and unlimited abundance and love.

Goal Affirmations

Repeat the following statements 21 consecutive times for 3 weeks.

I, [your name] _____ , am now ready and joyously accept the Great and Glorious Good that is entering my life.

I, _____ , have fearless faith that love, wealth, and happiness are mine and I welcome them into my life now.

I, _____ , now express a joyous Richness of spirit toward people. My Richness of spirit overflows and manifests material wealth in my life.

I, _____ , now attract all good things to me. I now meet just the right mate at just the right time for mutual joy in prosperity and happiness.

I, _____ , give myself complete and total permission as a perfect creation of the Father to experience the Richness of happiness, wealth, love, and marriage.

I, _____ , absolutely deserve prosperity and joyous love. I believe it is coming and I am thankful now.

I, _____ , now open myself—my heart, my mind, my daily life—to receive inflowing abundance from the universe in glorious love and prosperity.

I, _____ , now manifest a rich consciousness and draw to me a like consciousness in others. I draw to me those who have a Rich awareness and manifest material wealth.

I, _____ , readily accept my full and complete worthiness. I deserve love and wealth in a joyous relationship.

I, _____ , excitedly accept my glorious Good now coming to pass.

I, _____ , readily accept glorious good times, radiant happiness, and prosperity in health, love, and finances.

I, _____ , have a right heart and mind that sees and expects all good and joy in people and acknowledge my purest joy now comes to pass.

I, _____ , now expect sudden opportunities and recognize each with fearless faith and great gladness for the pleasure and fulfillment it abounds.

I, _____ , will meet many new and exciting people and race forward to new and thrilling adventures that bring richness and love ever more fully into my life.

As you read through the Positive Self-Reprogramming Statements, choose those that instantly have meaning to you. You don't have to say them all. Some of them may have meaning for you at a different time and you will use those at that time.

When you choose a statement, write it out 21 times first. Then, tape-record yourself saying it three different ways in the following sample:

I, Ginie Polo Sayles, am now ready and joyously accept the Great and Glorious Good that is entering my life.

You, Ginie Polo Sayles, are now ready and joyously accept the Great and Glorious Good that is entering your life.

She, Ginie Polo Sayles, is now ready and she joyously accept the Great and Glorious Good that is entering her life.

Record each one straight through in these 3 ways once. At night, when you go to bed, listen to it with your eyes closed. It's fine if you go to sleep listening to it, too. You will be hearing this reinforcement in the 3 ways you are used to hearing yourself referred to.

VISUALIZATION

I don't use visualization very much—although I must say that any time we think about the future with an idea of what we would like to have happen, our visualization process kicks in.

If you want to use visualization, fine. In my book *How to Win Pageants*, I point out that many national pageant winners, such as Miss America 1990, Gretchen Carlson, utilized visualization as a tool for winning.

Many successful athletes and sports competitors utilize visualization. Your brain often programs in the image you desire as if you have attained it and doesn't differentiate between what you have done and what you haven't.

Don't make a religious doctrine out of either affirmations or visualization. You can get into kooky stuff easily, and also into following a guru who puts you through paces of adoration for the guru and the guru's goals.

Instead, look at both affirmations and visualization as educational tools. They are somewhat scientific methods used often by psychologists to help you focus on goals.

They are methods to help you set your own programming for what you want. Viewing it that way, you'll have a healthy success with it.

All such tools are to be used to illuminate a richer Inner Richness in you so that you deserve the wealth in love and marriage that you seek.

INNER RICHNESS INCLUDES RESPONSIBILITY

In his book, *How To Be Rich*, J. Paul Getty said "that in our . . . society, too much emphasis was placed on *getting* rich . . ." that "little . . . attention was being paid to the important question of how to *be* rich . . . how to discharge the responsibilities created by wealth while enjoying the privileges . . . of it."

In the book, Getty goes on to say that "Richness is as much a matter of character, of philosophy, of outlook, and attitude, as it is of money."

Getty says that the "Millionaire mentality cannot be merely accumulative . . . that the ambitious who strive for success must know how to *be* rich in every positive sense of the term."

Responsibility, Not Morality

This book is not a book on morals. It tells you how to get what you want. However, you'll be more successful if you understand and adopt a few Old Guard values. And, if you do, you'll also *deserve* to marry the Rich.

The social Rich believe their money entitles them to the best in life and that it also obligates them to "give back" to society some of the Richness that our form of society has allowed them to acquire.

They do this through volunteer work, through large-scale charity fund-raising events, and through various foundations and donations.

History has shown that when a civilization is at its highest and best, there is a flourishing of art in all its forms—literature, painting, sculpture, dance, music, theater, and other innovations. There is also development in mathematics and the sciences.

The Rich consider it a duty to further civilization by becoming patrons to artists, and financial supporters of scientific research. The Rich think of themselves as pace-setters of respectability.

IS THIS NECESSARY FOR A RICH MARRIAGE?

You can marry an RM without these values, true; but to fully enjoy the Richness of self that money can afford you, you will want to make yourself over from the inside out, with values that include responsibility to society at large and to your RM.

And, mercenary though you are, you would never abandon an RM facing financial crisis who has befriended you with both his dollar and his name.

Even in the face of a scandal, you stand beside your RM—man or woman—until the crisis subsides. After the crisis, you can leave if you want to. You will have the respect of other RMs who witnessed or heard of your strength of character. This can enhance your chances of a future with other RMs.

It is worthwhile to develop these values that contribute to Richness of self because external objects are meaningless in and of themselves, if they are not used to express a fine inner quality of respect for life, love, beauty, and kindness.

It is only what each object represents to us, individually and socially, and from the frame of reference we have, that gives it value at all.

You want money because of the luxurious trappings it provides, yes; and you also want it because it sets you free to become the best you that you can be—to develop yourself, to express yourself, and to elevate life for others in ways you never could have before you married your RM.

Yes, it *is* just as easy to earn the Riches yourself; but by the time you've married your RM, you *have* earned it yourself! You've worked hard to become the best and most prized asset to an RM of all his or her assets.

Besides, even if you do earn Riches on your own, there is still the problem of finding a mate who shares your monetary and new social values. It is *efficient* to resolve your romantic and your financial needs in one contract—marriage.

You can still pursue a career and make a fortune yourself before, during, and after you've married your RM.

You can and should judge people by their hearts and not their money. At the same time, you should be aware that sex, love, and money are the dynamics of any marriage relationship and that *the Rich are going to marry somebody, why not YOU?*

Send for a FREE list of products
by

Ginie Polo Sayles

Write to
Ginie Polo Sayles
P.O. Box 460194
Houston, Texas 77056-8194

And **REMEMBER**

Ginie gives seminars around the country. Write to her, requesting a schedule of when she will be in your area.

OR

Your group or organization may schedule Ginie for a seminar or class. Send for more information today! Ginie also offers limited numbers of private group seminars and limited one-on-one private consultations.

Request information at the address above.